The Kaye Berreano Mystery Series, Book 2: Safe House

By Christine Duncan

Writers Exchange E-Publishing

http://www.writers-exchange.com

The Kay Berreano Mystery Series, Book 2: Safe House

Contents

Chapter 1 1

Chapter 2 11

Chapter 3 19

Chapter 4 27

Chapter 5 39

Chapter 6 49

Chapter 7 56

Chapter 8 65

Chapter 9 73

Chapter 10 85

Chapter 11 96

Chapter 12 104

Chapter 13 115

Chapter 14 126

Chapter 15 141

Chapter 16 155

Chapter 17 171

Chapter 18 189

Chapter 19 202

Chapter 20 208

About the Author...214

The Kaye Berreano Mystery Series 215

Chapter 1

Something was wrong.

It was rush hour, literally freezing and snow was piling up all over the front range. Most sensible Coloradoans were driving carefully home from work and huddling in for the night. Or at least driving to the grocery store, and stocking up before they huddled in.

Yet the same street lamp, which illuminated blowing snow and cast eerie shadows off the leafless trees in front of the recreation center, clearly showed a large crowd milling on the sidewalk under the trees in spite of the cold.

Something was definitely wrong. And my fourteen-year-old son, RJ, was here.

Hurriedly, I steered my car into the parking lot of the suburban Denver recreation center and pulled up to the curb, ignoring the parking slots. Then I jumped out, not even bothering to close the car door.

Teens with basketballs stood silently, their faces sullen. Little kids, who shouldn't have been out in the darkness of the early November evening snowstorm, leaned on their bikes watching. Parents come to pick up their own kids, obvious in their suits topped by heavy coats, rimmed the crowd, faces set in a universal frown of disapproval. A couple of red-jacketed Rec center employees stood toward the crowd's middle.

I bolted through the blowing snow toward them, unable to see anything over the heads of the silent crowd.

"Where is she?" A woman's voice, angry and loud.

A male voice answered, but it was so muffled I couldn't make it out.

"You know. I know you do," the woman screeched. "If you don't tell me, I'll...."

"You're losing it. What's your problem?" The second voice was loud now and made no attempt to hide its owner's disgust.

Oh God.

"If we could just settle this inside, quietly." One of the rec. center clerks gestured to the glass doors of the gym.

"No!" the woman in the center of it all blared.

What was going on? I moved closer, standing on tiptoe to see over the heads of the crowd. Who was talking to RJ that way? And why?

The woman, her dark curls mussed, her face streaked with tears, lunged toward RJ, grabbed him by the shoulders and shook him.

That was all I needed to see. I pushed my way in, yelling, "Stop that."

I was so intent on RJ and the woman that without meaning to, I bumped into a little blond boy--no more than eight--on his bike.

"Ooh," he said, bike teetering precariously.

I steadied the bike and looked at the boy quickly to make sure he was okay. Then my own son claimed my attention with another shout, and I pushed deeper into the crowd.

I ploughed past a glowering basketball player, his sweatshirt stained with perspiration. From there, I had a clear view, although I was still not free of the crowd.

RJ braced himself against the woman's grasp, making his six-foot tall, skinny body rigid under her onslaught. His loose black jeans, T-shirt, and his short dark hair flopped in time to her jolting. He had no way to defend himself. I'd taught him never to hit a woman.

I had no such inhibitions. If I got my hands on her, I'd deck her for messing with my kid. I could, too, even though she looked to be at least five foot seven and I was only five two. She was probably younger, too. But she was model thin and I had taken up kickboxing for my fortieth birthday.

I pushed my way past the last kid, and plunged in between the woman and RJ. Only when I had actually grabbed her by her navy, cashmere blazer and hauled her physically off my son, did I realize that the woman attacking RJ was a friend - Thea Pappas.

"Kaye," she gasped and then burst out crying, leaning on my shoulder as though she were the one who'd been attacked and I was her savior.

This woman had been our neighbor for twenty years. Our kids had grown up together, and I'd never seen her even yell at one of my kids before. I'd never seen her yell period, let alone physically assault someone.

The urge to avenge my son leaked out of me. I put a protective arm around her sobbing form. "What is going on?" Bewildered, I looked from my son to the crowd.

"Don't ask me, Mom," RJ said, picking up a black hooded sweatshirt from where it had dropped on the ground, and pulling it over his head. "She just went off on me."

One of the clerks stepped forward. She was a mousy little thing, probably not much past high school, wearing khakis that might have been maternity slacks. "We were called out here because of the disturbance. We thought it was a family thing-- but you're his mother?"

I could understand why she would question it. RJ got his height, his blue eyes and his always-neat dark hair from his dad. I hastily combed through my own short brown curls with my fingers, before I realized my other arm still held a weeping Thea, her tears soaking through my sweater.

I spared a rueful thought for my dry-cleaning bill. "Yes, RJ is my son," I said to the clerk. "I'm Kaye Berreano."

Thea straightened and stepped back from me. "You're not Atchinson anymore?"

I shook my head. "I took back my maiden name with the divorce."

The clerk hugged herself, shivering against the wind that blew stinging blasts of snow. "Ladies, can we go in and straighten this out?"

I nodded and, lock-stepped by necessity with Thea who kept a tight grasp on me, I moved toward the glass doors. RJ and the clerks trailed. The teenaged crowd fell back before the adults, but out of the corner of my eye, I saw a couple of boys step forward to give RJ a comforting punch on the arm before he went in.

When we got inside, the clerks took the lead, the older one showing us a door in the short green corridor that lead toward an office off the gym. The glare of fluorescent lights bounced off three gray metal desks.

Pulling a couple of wheeled secretarial chairs out into a circle, the young, mousy clerk looked indecisively at the older one who cleared her throat and shook her head.

"As long as there will be no further problems, we'll leave you alone to solve this," said the mouse.

I nodded. "Don't worry. I'm sure this is all a misunderstanding." I shot a meaningful look at Thea and then my son.

Thea stared vacantly at an announcement of upcoming classes posted on the lime-colored wall. She was obviously consumed by her own thoughts. I guided her to a chair and, when she got to it, she looked at it as though she didn't know what it was. Then, slowly, she lowered herself into it.

All of this was too strange. First, she attacked my son and now she seemed almost withdrawn into herself. Waiting only for the clerks to shut the door, I said, "Will one of you please tell me what is going on?"

RJ shrugged his skinny shoulders. "I told you, she went off on me. I don't know why."

"Thea?"

She continued looking off, but her voice showed the emotion her blank face didn't. "I have to find out what happened to Elissa. RJ knows that."

"What about Elissa?"

Thea wouldn't look at me. RJ did, and raised his brows as if to say, *see what I mean.* I could question RJ later--when he couldn't escape. But even though he was the one Thea had been shaking out in the parking lot, I doubted she'd tell me much in front of him-or anyone else. I watched her quietly and made up my mind. To RJ, I said, "Why don't you go find wherever it is you left your backpack and wait for me out at the car?"

He glanced down at his hands as though expecting to find the backpack dangling off them, then he looked up at me and Thea. His mouth curved up in a quick nervous smile, which was replaced by lowered brows and a pursed look around the mouth, also quickly wiped from his face. "I, uh, must have left it at Zack's."

I knew from his face that he hadn't, of course, but it was just another thing to deal with later. "Okay, go ask Zack about it, if he's still here. Maybe we can swing by later. Then just wait for me in the car."

The door banged shut behind him. I sat slowly down on the edge of my chair.

"Thea," I said quietly, "do you want to tell me what this is all about?"

She turned toward me, her huge dark eyes confused now. "Have you seen Elissa? She said she was meeting Hannah down here."

The anger and confusion seemed so odd. It was almost as though Thea were in a state of shock. "No.... I'm here to pick up RJ. Hannah's choral group is on a trip to Pueblo today. I didn't think the girls saw much of each other anymore."

Thea's face tightened. "I should have known. Elissa said Hannah didn't have any time for her since you and Roger divorced. But I'm sure Hannah told you."

"Hannah said that she and Elissa didn't hang out with the same crowd now." I shrugged and smiled. "I figured, maybe it was the age difference. You know, a year's a lot at their ages and Hannah is fifteen now."

"You mean Hannah said she didn't like the kids Elissa hangs out with."

Actually Hannah had been much more graphic, complaining about the skaters and Goths that Elissa hung out with. I didn't want to meet Thea's eyes. "Pretty much."

Thea shook her head. "One of the ladies in the office thinks she saw Elissa about two hours ago with a couple of kids, but she's gone."

"Was RJ one of the kids?"

Thea shrugged, and slumped back against her chair, her voice husky with unshed tears.

"Thea, why did you shake RJ?"

"The thing is Elissa has been doing this kind of thing lately."

Why wouldn't she just answer me? "What kind of thing has Elissa been doing? You mean not showing up where she tells you she's going to be?"

Thea's mouth twisted. Tears trickled unchecked down her cheeks. "That and running away. This summer she'd only come home to sleep a couple of days and pick up some clean clothes then she'd be off again."

Elissa? She was so young. But I knew from looking at Thea that it was true. I'd seen enough of this kind of thing and not just in the course of my counseling career. It meant drugs, usually. Even Arvada, a Denver suburb, wasn't immune anymore. Still Thea and her husband were pretty savvy; they had probably thought of that. "Does she say why?"

"She's gotten into a crowd that does that. Most of them are older-- eighteen, or nineteen I'd guess. They stay away for days, and party--you know--drugs and alcohol. Then when they need to come down, they go home to sleep it off--until the next party."

Even though the answer was no more than I expected, I felt shocked and saddened. "Have you talked to her about it?"

"Oh, yes." Thea's tired voice told its own story. "She says, 'Mom, I'm not your little girl anymore. I'm going out, and I'm going to have fun, and there's nothing you can do about it.'"

"Do you call her in as a runaway when she goes off like that?"

"For all the good that does."

The police did what they could but there were only so many cops. I nodded. "How about a drug program? There's an excellent..."

Thea shook her head. "The court put her in one a few months back. They kept her in-house for three weeks, and then she had six weeks outpatient. If you ask me, she just learned more about where to get drugs and how to hide them. As soon as she got out, she left. We didn't see her again for weeks."

The court--that meant Elissa had been arrested, and they wouldn't do that just for running away. I kept my face straight, something I'd learned how to do on my job at the battered women's shelter. I could understand why Thea was upset, if she thought Elissa was off to another drug party.

I felt pretty bad myself. This girl had been my daughter's best friend. I'd fed her cookies and milk after school, had her over for sleepovers, and birthday parties. "What can I do for you?"

Thea twisted her mouth into a smile and shook her head, blinking back her tears. "Nothing, Kaye. She's probably just run away again. I'm sorry for crying on your shoulder. But I don't think there's anything you can do."

* * *

RJ and I sat silently in the car, not talking much at first, mostly because RJ didn't talk unless I asked him something directly.

I felt too distracted by what had happened with Thea to make my usual inquiries about school. I'd driven halfway home before I even realized that Thea had never really told me why she was shaking RJ. What did she think RJ knew about Elissa?

I looked over at RJ. "What went on back there?"

RJ's figure appeared collapsed inside his black sweatshirt and jeans. He was so skinny that with his head fallen forward on his chest like that he looked like nothing more than a pile of clothes in the seat next to me. "I told you. I don't know."

When had this sulky teenager replaced my son? He used to be so sweet. Hormones! I tightened my mouth, and glared sideways at him.

He watched me silently, apparently sizing up my reaction correctly because he abruptly sat up. "'Lissa's mom thought I knew where 'Lissa was. But I don't know why. I kept saying I wasn't hanging out with her today."

I turned onto Kipling Street to find a sea of headlights. I barely cleared the intersection before I had to stop. Luckily, we had only a couple of blocks to go before home. "Do you hang out with her a lot?"

He hunched a shoulder.

I took that as a yes. "You never said anything."

"It was no big deal. I see her around sometimes." RJ's voice revealed that the subject bored him, but he was still carefully friendly.

"RJ, where did she go?"

"I wasn't hanging around with her today, Mom. We were playing basketball."

The traffic situation could have been annoying, but it worked to my advantage just then. I could afford to swing around and face him. I took his chin in my hand so I could watch his eyes. "I didn't ask if you hung with her. I asked if you knew where she went," I said softly.

RJ didn't allow me to touch him in public and everything outside of his goodnight kiss had been declared public. So I fully expected he would shrug out from under my hand. Instead he shook his head at me, wide-eyed. What was going on?

Behind me, sirens blared. I groaned. That must be the problem. An accident up ahead. There was nowhere I could go to move over for the approaching ambulance.

The ambulance went briefly up the wrong side of the road, prompting visions of a head-on collision, before it swerved onto the median strip. Then at the top, where the grass ended for a center turn lane, the ambulance swung over and disappeared from my view.

I let out a sigh of relief. At least the rescue crew wasn't going to be cremated in my sight. I turned back to RJ.

"If you saw Elissa, why didn't you tell Thea?"

RJ's neck was still craned for a glimpse of the ambulance even though he couldn't possibly see it anymore. He broke out of his trance reluctantly. "She already knew Elissa left."

"Elissa left when?"

"I don't know, Mom." The sulk was back in his voice. "I wasn't keeping track. I saw her when we started, but when we were working on our hook shots, she was gone."

"Did you see who she went with?" I could still hear the sirens. The accident must be just up the hill. Traffic started to inch forward though, and I needed to keep my eyes on the road now. So I wasn't looking when RJ replied.

"Just some people--nobody you know."

The mother part of me filed the fact that he knew these people, and didn't want me to know. His voice told me that much. And that scared me-

-considering what Thea had just said about Elissa's friends. But it was time for me to get off his back. I'd learn more if I waited and kept my eyes open.

Besides traffic picked up. I passed the spot where the ambulance had parked opposite us on the grassy side of the road. Though I squinted hard as I went by, I couldn't see any cars. Dark as it was out there, that didn't surprise me. Someone must have slid off the side of the road and crashed.

Chapter 2

I tried phoning Thea the next morning before work, but got no answer. All I really wanted was to make sure it had all turned out okay. Sighing, I set the phone back down and finished dressing for work. I had a counseling session with one of the residents of the battered women's shelter scheduled for ten.

Thea's anguished face still haunted me as I climbed the steps to Beginning's peeling front porch. I knew how I would feel if it were Hannah. But what could I do? Resolutely, I pushed my friend from my mind, and reached for the door. It opened from the inside.

"Hi, Kaye," said my boss, Liz Windfield. Her short, graying, beige hair looked as though she'd been running her fingers through it, and her small figure drooped.

Had it been her night to work? And if so, why was she still here? She should have left by five-thirty. "Hey, Liz. I thought Dina was supposed to be on last night."

Liz wrinkled her nose. "She switched with me. The baby has a cold and she didn't want to leave him last night. Then she had to take him in to the pediatrician today, so she was late." Liz shrugged. "So much the better, she can cope with it today." With a tired wave, Liz went out the door.

Cope with what? At first glance, the large L-shaped room looked empty. But angry raised voices provided a clue to what Liz meant.

Around the corner of the room, I saw my coworker and two shelter residents, one in a blue, terry bathrobe, the other a short, heavy-set brunette dressed in jeans and a T-shirt.

"This woman is impossible," said the one in the robe.

"I'm impossible?" the brunette asked. "Dina, I can't believe this. I cannot put up with her constant mess, the late hours, the constant blaring of her boom box...."

I saw Dina's bleached blonde head nod. Catching her eye, I waved, then turned around toward the office to meet my client. Hopefully, mine would want to concentrate on her goals for her thirty-day stay here at Beginnings, instead of roommate troubles.

Coming in at ten always left me with the feeling that I had a 'parts' job. I did parts of whatever the other counselors couldn't get to. I didn't see the women eat breakfast, but I got to make sure that whoever was on cleanup did her bit. I had to make sure that the ordering was done for groceries, but I wasn't the one who made the list. I had some arrangements to make for the evening meeting for legal night but someone else would conduct it. In between the minutia, I also answered the phone, filled out paper work and did a little counseling.

Chores kept me busy until late afternoon, but Thea's face plagued me. I would feel better if I knew things were back to normal. I snuck in a couple of phone calls to her but I never connected. The woman was always busy. Hopefully she'd get my message and call back.

I stared vacantly at the weak, late-afternoon sunshine slanting in the tiny office window as I hung up the last time.

Dina came in and slumped down in one of the gray folding chairs, putting her elbows on the battered desk, and her chin in her hands. Her eyes were heavily lined with Kohl today, and her hands had some kind of henna tattoo.

"Liz said you had to take the baby to the doctor's this morning."

Dina's mouth did a quick turndown. "I lied. I didn't want to tell her that I was up all night with the baby and I just overslept. I didn't get here until 9:45 and I felt so guilty."

"Oops! What did Liz say?"

"She just asked if everything was all right. I told her I owed her big time."

I grinned. "So when is she collecting?"

"This weekend. One of the interns needs to study for an exam so I'll be here all night Saturday."

"Bet you'll make sure you hear the alarm next time."

Dina nodded. "Speaking of being late...."

I glanced at the clock. Almost five. "Oh, God, the happy hour meeting!"

I ran a comb through my hair and put on lipstick, resolving again not to think about Thea and Elissa. This meeting of shelter graduates was important. Woman often left the shelter to return to their abusers and this meeting was their chance to check in, and get help and education on the problem. One of the women I was expecting at the meeting tonight was in this category, and I had been planning to focus on her particularly--hoping to convince her to go to couple's counseling with him. I put on my coat and trudged out into the cold November air.

The previous night's six inches of snow crunched under my feet. One of the women had volunteered to shovel the back walk this week, but obviously she hadn't gotten to it yet. The lock to the garage turned meeting place/office was frozen enough to make it difficult to turn the key.

Like so much of the shelter, we furnished this meeting place with someone's garage sale leftovers. A scarred, fake-wood folding table stood on a green shag carpet remnant. Against the wall were a swivel chair and a steel desk, minus one drawer. Black metal folding chairs leaned up against the opposite wall. The heating was, to say the least, inadequate, so I kept my coat around my shoulders and turned on lights, switching the sign on the window to Welcome. I pulled out a small circle of folding chairs, then settled down to wait.

Carla Meyers was the first safehouse graduate to come in, stomping her feet to remove the snow from her worn boots, her caramel-colored hair falling in waves around her face.

"How's it going?" I asked.

She shrugged. "The kids are giving me a hard time. Jacob's cutting classes, and Adrienne's grades have dropped."

Carla's four teenagers were the reason she'd finally decided to leave her husband. But kids had their own reactions to domestic violence and divorce. I sighed. A thirty-day stay at the shelter couldn't begin to help with everything. That was why we held these meetings.

Nicky Greenwood burst in the door, a gust of cold air coming with her. Quickly she removed her cloche hat, leaving her fine dark hair full of static. She shivered as she peeled off her black leather jacket with cold-reddened fingers. She looked frail and tired for someone who was just turned twenty. Maybe just the effort to keep up with three kids under five.

"Hi, Nicky," I said. To Carla, I said, "It's hard on the kids, too."

Nicky was the one to respond. "Hard? Is that what you said? Tell me about it. Hard is going to work on the bus, and dropping your kids off at daycare on the way. It takes me two hours to get to work in the morning-- because of all the stinking buses I gotta catch."

I scanned her slight figure with concern. She'd lost weight since the baby was born, prematurely, due to her knife-wielding boyfriend. No surprise there. She'd lost so much blood in the attack, the baby was ready to leave the hospital well before Nicky.

"It is a tough schedule," I said, nodding at her. "I bet you'll be glad to graduate that training program, so you can find a job a little closer to home."

She shrugged and plopped herself down in the middle of the circle of chairs. "I'll be glad to make enough money to afford a car."

The door opened again. The last straggler dragged herself through. I swiveled my chair toward the doorway to greet the newcomer, the woman who I had been the most worried about. "So how's it going, Anita?"

Anita Conners turned her ruddy face toward me and brushed her tangle of strawberry blonde hair out of her eyes to stare as though surprised by my question. "Okay." In a more forceful voice, she said, "It's going all right." She peeled off her coat to reveal a shapeless, orange dress that clashed with her complexion and made her figure look dumpy.

"Yeah, right," said Nicky. "Has he agreed to counseling yet?"

I could have kissed her for asking.

"No." Anita drew the word out as she pulled a folding chair off the wall, and inserted it into our circle. She said brightly, "But we haven't had any problems."

Carla snorted, and leaned her skinny body forward to put her tanned cat's face into Anita's. "Next time you go bopping out of there to the safehouse again--make sure you don't go back until he agrees to counseling."

I shifted in my hard chair and kicked off my pumps. "Amen."

"Better yet." Nicky said, fingering the still reddened scars on her hands that she'd gotten from defending herself from her man. "Get out now while you can and don't look back."

I looked at Nicky, meeting her big brown eyes, "You're not going back then?"

"Do I look stupid?" she asked.

"It isn't stupid to want things to work out," said Anita. "Is it, Kaye?"

I sighed and took my time to answer, trying to keep my own biases in check. I wanted to be able to save her from the revolving door so many of these women went through. They'd leave, the guy would promise the moon, then they'd go back and nothing would be different. And every time a woman went back without anything being different, she was in danger. "The question isn't whether it's stupid. Feelings are never stupid or smart. But is it realistic? Does he want to work things out with you?"

"He loves me."

Nicky leaned forward in her seat, her huge dark eyes burning fiercely against her thin, white face. "He loves you, but don't expect him to go to counseling." She waved impatiently at Anita. "Hello! Can't you see what he's telling you?"

Anita shrugged her shoulders. "It's not the same as you, Nicky. He never put me in the hospital or anything. He just gets angry. And it doesn't happen that often."

"He gets angry, and he hits you," Carla said quietly but with all the authority of someone who really knew. "He doesn't have to put you in the hospital for it to be abuse. Don't you understand?"

"You don't understand. I'm not one of you feminists." Anita looked down at her lap, her long bright hair hiding her face. I could tell from her voice that she was crying. "I've got a son who I don't want to raise on my own. My parents were divorced, and I swore up and down that I would never get divorced. I want my son to grow up to know his dad." She looked up, tears streaming down her cheeks. Her whole face was blotchy red with emotion and her nose was running.

This had been going on too long. Anita needed to hear the point. I passed her a tissue from the box we kept on the desk for just such a time. "This is something you've thought about a lot," I said, in what I hoped was a calming voice.

"Of course," Anita said, wiping under her eyes.

"But you haven't thought it all through. He's hurting you. That's abuse. And that's not good for your son or you."

"Listen to me," Anita's voice was loud as though to drown me out. "I ... don't... want... a ... divorce."

"What makes you think that counseling means a divorce?" I kept my own voice at a low level, but I needed to know. How had I given that message?

"Look at these women." Anita waved her arm around the circle. "Nicky's not going back--ever. Carla filed her divorce papers while she was still in the safe house. Even you're divorced, Kaye."

The reaction was instantaneous and loud. "That doesn't mean we advocate divorce," I stated.

Nicky said, "I can at least see..."

Carla's voice won out over all. "I didn't want a divorce, Anita," Carla said, eyes shining with tears. "He wouldn't take me back. He had somebody else. If it had been up to me, I'd have gone to counseling with that man, and fought for my marriage."

Of course, it was tiny, whirlwind Nicky who reached over and hugged Carla to her. I passed along the tissue box.

Anita's eyes were wide and anguished. Her own tears dried on her cheeks as she considered Carla in surprise. "I'm sorry. I didn't know."

"No, you don't know, girl," Carla said. In her upset, her voice took on an accent I'd heard only traces of before. "You come into this place, and instead of tryin' to learn somethin', you act like you got it all figured out from the get go. Nobody here's been sayin' 'get a divorce, Anita.' All we're sayin' is--he's abusin' you. You act like you're not sure 'bout that. Get sure. I'm here to tell you he's abusin' you. And you're not doin' anything about it."

"I left." Anita sounded indignant now.

Nicky patted Carla's hand then shifted back in her own chair restlessly. "Yeah, you left. Then he said come back, so you went back. You think you spending a couple of days in the shelter changes anything? You didn't change nothing."

Anita said, "I tr--"

Nicky cut her off with a wave of her hand. "Don't you even tell us you tried. I've seen you here before. If just leaving worked, why didn't it work the first time then? Why didn't it work for me, or her?" Nicky pointed at Carla. "You didn't try. You just came here to whine, and now you're pissed 'cause we won't let you."

Carla finished wiping her nose with the tissue and said tiredly. "You want it to work. Go ahead. Work at it. That's all we're sayin'."

I nodded at her in approval then turned back to Anita. "You can't turn your back on this. Domestic violence has a cycle. Things might be okay right now. But it will happen again. You need to face that, watch for the signs, and figure out what you want to do."

Anita's whole body shuddered; the anger she'd nursed at us draining out of her. She looked white and exhausted. "He won't go to counseling. He told me that. He said all they do there is blame everything on the man."

"Poor baby!" said Nicky. "Don't we feel sorry for him? What should we blame on you? You're not hitting him, are you?"

"So I should just leave him, even though everything's going okay right now, because he won't go to counseling? This doesn't feel right."

"What do feelings have to do with doin' right?" Carla whispered. "What about what you're teachin' that son of yours? How are you goin' to feel when he starts hittin' people? How are you goin' to feel when your daughter-in-law comes and tells you he hits her?"

"All right. All right. I heard you. All of you." Anita stood up and struggled back into her gray coat. "I've got to think." She shook her head. "I'm not like you. I can't just make a decision to leave like this. I've got to think."

Chapter 3

I made my way through rush hour traffic and turned toward my house on the west side of town, more than ready for a quiet night--as soon as I talked to Thea. A vaguely familiar green Ford F150 stood at the curb of my little ranch house, blocking my way in.

Blast it. I couldn't even drive into my own driveway. I spied three more cars in front of my neighbor's and made myself take a deep breath. They were nice people. I didn't want to bang on their door to ask their guest to move his truck. Irritably, I reversed my Volvo and parked in back of the Ford.

Collecting purse, keys, and papers, I dragged myself up the sloping walk. It was dark, and the walk was slick with patches of ice because, of course, I had shoveled after we walked on it.

The door stuck a little, then a gust of warm air and thumping music met me. The living room stood empty. The hardwood floor gleamed in the light spilling from the kitchen. Backpacks, coats and sweatshirts covered the two blue- and sand-colored couches and their matching chairs. Obviously, RJ and Hannah had made it home. Not that I needed additional proof, the rock music that vibrated the wood floor was enough.

The smell of onions and meat cooking wafted through the air. I sighed hopefully. Could it be Hannah's night to cook? RJ was getting better. He'd graduated from spaghetti and tacos to a few basic casseroles. But Hannah could really cook--no thanks to me. She'd inherited my mother's and, give the devil his due, my ex-husband Roger's talent in that direction. On the nights that it was my turn to cook, I cranked out the food and looked forward to a night off. I really preferred our Friday take-out nights, and so, I'm sure, did the kids.

"What's for dinner?" I called.

"RJ's making burritos," said Hannah, popping her head out of the kitchen.

I wrinkled my nose, and then tried to smile, setting my stuff down so I could hang my coat in the closet.

"Can you turn that down?" I waved toward the boom box in the corner.

She flipped the switch on the music and stepped closer to whisper something in my ear. Since my arm was half in and half out of my coat, I backed away to avoid hitting her. I kept my eyes on her as I hung up the coat.

At fifteen, she didn't usually pay much attention when I walked in the door. A casual "hi, mom" yelled from the other room was the most I usually got. But her face looked flushed and she caught her bottom lip between her teeth guiltily. Something was up.

"Is something the matter?" I asked.

"Nooo." Hannah shook her head at me violently, her whole body jiggling with the effort. She got her height, or lack of it, from me, the blond hair came from Roger's mom. The dimples were from me, too, but the small, even, white teeth were Roger's. Her green eyes were all her own. In other words, the kid got the best of both of us and improved on it. She was gorgeous, and that wasn't just a mom talking either.

But she was trying to tell me something, and I couldn't figure out what. "What's the deal then?"

"Your daughter is trying to prepare you for the idea that I'm here," said Pete Farrell leaning against the kitchen doorway. He looked pretty comfortable for someone who had only been in my house only once and that time months before. He'd been the investigator for a fire at Beginnings and had come to ask me questions. Later, when all the questions on the fire were answered, we started dating.

I pressed my eyes closed. But when I opened them again, he was still there. I took in details, gathering additional proof. He looked good, his lean frame clothed in gray slacks and a blue shirt, his graying red hair a little mussed. He cocked his head, assessing my reaction. His blue eyes twinkled at my surprise. It was definitely him all right. He seemed to think this was a good joke. At least that explained the pickup out front. No wonder I'd thought it was familiar. But he wasn't supposed to be here.

"I thought we'd agreed that it would be better if we kept our relationship away from my kids," I said stiffly.

His smile was affable, friendly--charming even. "You said that," he conceded.

I moved to a chair, brushing the assorted clothing to the floor, and sat down, aware of his eyes on me the whole time. "I thought you agreed."

He shook his head, still smiling. "I told you I thought it was time the kids and I met."

I turned my head toward Hannah, feeling irrationally angry. RJ squeaked through the doorway behind Pete, and came to stand by his sister. His dark hair looked rumpled, his black pants sported patches that he said were his favorite bands. So why did their names have to be obscene? I hated that.

That kid and I argued constantly about his wardrobe. Still, that was hardly the point at the moment.

"Do you always let strangers in the house?" I asked.

Hannah rolled her eyes. "Mom, it's been months. It's not like we didn't know you were dating."

"Geeze, you act like we're stupid or something," RJ chimed in.

Obviously, I wouldn't get any help there. I turned to Pete. "I think you should leave."

"Why?" His freckled face expressed honest bewilderment. "I'm a nice person. Your kids aren't going to be contaminated by being around me." Pete pushed off the doorjamb to stand over me. He reached lazily down to stroke my hair. "Why can't I stay?"

The phone shrilled in the background. Both my kids went running, leaving me to answer a question that I had apparently already flubbed. I looked up, deep into Pete's blue eyes.

"RJ, you jerk, give me that phone," Hannah squealed.

Saved by the phone wars. I brushed irritably at my hair and stood up, squeezing around his body. "Look, this isn't the time. I want to talk to you about this some more, but not here." I walked across the room, a safe distance from his tempting presence.

"RJ, I swear to God if you don't give me that phone, I'm going to..."

"RJ, give your sister the phone," I roared, taking out my frustration with Pete on my kid.

RJ danced back into the room, smiling. "Nobody in this house can take a joke."

From the kitchen, Hannah said loudly into the phone, "I know. He is sooo annoying."

"You better not be talking about me, stupid," RJ yelled.

Pete walked over to me and started massaging my shoulders. I decided to ignore him. I glared at my son, making sure to look him straight in the eye, so he could have no doubt that I meant it. "RJ, that's enough."

Over my shoulder, Pete asked, "How are those burritos going? That's not what I smell burning, is it?"

"I forgot." RJ dashed out of the room.

Pete's hands were warm on my shoulders. The massage felt good. Too good. I wanted to melt. Ignoring Pete wasn't working in the way I'd thought it would. I had to take the time to talk while my family circus had an intermission. I didn't want to, though.

"Pete, you have to stop." I reached up and grabbed his hands from my shoulders, then twisted around to face him. "I mean it. I've given this a lot of thought. My kids have been through enough with this divorce. They don't need to meet every guy I date and then be hurt when he's gone."

He smiled at me, blue eyes crinkling at the corners. He looked straight into my eyes. "That was good thinking on your part. You're a good mother."

He understood. I smiled.

"There's just one problem. I'm not just some guy you're dating and I'm not going anywhere. I've told you how I feel, and I'm tired of meeting you at coffee shops or when your kids are at their dad's."

My heart thumped so loudly and so fast, I felt sure he could hear it. I looked down at our hands, still intertwined. I laced and unlaced my fingers through his as I tried to think how to phrase what I wanted to say. I knew I'd been less than fair with him. He'd told me up front he was looking for a serious relationship. And lately he'd been more than hinting about getting married. I loved the guy, but I hadn't even been divorced a year. "Look, I'm not..."

"RJ, I swear to God, I've had enough. You'd better watch it." Hannah's whisper could be heard across town.

This didn't sound like part of the phone wars. What had happened that I missed?

The phone rang again. I disengaged myself from Pete and walked into the kitchen. RJ stood over the stove, busily stirring the meat in the fry pan, eyes glued to his task. Hannah held the phone out to me.

"What's going on?"

Hannah looked at me, then turned her gaze deliberately to Pete who had followed me into the kitchen. I glanced back at him. He raised an eyebrow and turned back toward RJ.

"Hey, RJ, did you add any cayenne?" he asked.

One of the best things about Pete was his intelligence.

I turned my back on the guys, and stepped closer to Hannah and the phone. "What's going on?" I repeated in a lower voice.

"Mom, it's the phone." Hannah sounded annoyed.

I shook my head and tightened my mouth. Later. Definitely. Hannah shook her head back at me, handed me the phone and flounced out of the kitchen.

"Kaye?" The voice seemed familiar, but I couldn't place it. The line crackled loudly in my ear. "This is Thea Pappas, returning your call."

"Oh, hi, Thea. The reason I called is that I wanted to see how everything turned out with Elissa." I felt conscious of sounding artificially bright and cheerful--a response to the ominous calm in her voice.

Pete must have noticed. He turned away from RJ and the stove to watch me. Then crossing his arms over his chest, he came over to stand beside me.

"They found her," Thea said.

"That's good." My voice betrayed my uncertainty. It should be good, but it didn't sound like it. Who found her?

"Kaye, she's dead." Thea's voice broke, and I heard the muffled sound of her sobs. In the background, there were voices, but I couldn't make any of them out.

"I don't understand," I said slowly. "What happened?"

RJ turned away from the stove and watched me, frowning. Hannah crept back in the kitchen. Pete pulled me to him, so that my back rested against his chest. And I let him, dimly aware that doing so made the kids watch even more wide-eyed.

"I don't know what happened," wailed Thea. "I put in the runaway report after we got done talking yesterday." She sniffed. "So then, the police called me last night to tell me that they'd gotten a call about a problem at Kipling and Ralston. When they got there, it was just a field and it looked empty. But they looked around and they found a girl."

Kipling and Ralston? The ambulance I'd seen last night? My God! My throat closed tightly. It made sense though. It was walking distance from the Rec center. "What happened?"

I heard Thea swallow and make a shuddering sound as though she had taken a deep breath to try to control her tears. "The man on the phone--he was really kind--he said..." Thea sniffed again, and cleared her throat. "They didn't know if she was my daughter or not. Her clothing and age and all matched the description I'd given, but she didn't have any ID on her. Then he asked if I could please come down and identify her."

"Oh, my God."

"Yes. Kaye, it's been awful."

What could I say? This was every parent's worst nightmare. "I'm so sorry."

"The hardest part is I can't get the picture of her eyes out of my head. Those big eyes of hers just said, 'Mom, help me'."

"So she was alive when you got there? You got to be with her before she died."

"No, I...." Thea paused, and I heard a rummaging sound. "Sorry, I couldn't find any tissue." She exhaled a shaking breath, and said in a high trembling voice. "Yes, I saw her. I kept hoping that this was a dream or something--that it wasn't really happening." Thea's voice dissolved into tears. "But it happened. My baby's dead."

Chapter 4

Hannah broke the silence in the kitchen, her voice anxious. "Mom, that wasn't Elissa's mom, was it?"

I nodded, my throat tightly closed. How could I tell the kids? How much did they get from hearing my side of the conversation?

"What happened?"

I shook my head, tears burning my eyes. "Honey, they don't know yet. RJ and I saw Thea at the Rec center looking for Elissa last night. Thea was upset."

Hannah waved a hand. "RJ told me last night. Just tell us, Mom."

I nodded. "Okay. 911 apparently got an anonymous call about a problem going on in a field over by Kipling Street. The cops arrived." I cleared my throat, looking around for tissues myself.

Pete grabbed a napkin from a holder on the table and handed it to me, then came back to massage my shoulders.

I looked up at him gratefully. "Thea and Elissa Pappas used to be our neighbors." I nodded at my daughter. "Hannah grew up with Elissa."

He nodded, his face grave. "If I were as nice as I keep trying to tell you, I'd offer to leave. But I'm afraid you'd take me up on it."

I opened my mouth ready to say what a good idea that was, when he put his fingers on my lips. "Talk to your kids. I'll be here." He turned me firmly around and started massaging my shoulders again.

RJ's face looked set. He returned my look blankly. Hannah's shoulders were rigid, her face white. They both knew something bad was coming. Better to get this over with.

"Anyway," I said. "By the time the cops arrived, everyone but one girl was gone, and she was unconscious. They took her to the hospital." I looked carefully from RJ to Hannah, unsure what to say. I didn't know much--not even really how Elissa had died. Grateful for Pete's warm hands on my shoulders, I picked my words carefully.

"The cops didn't know who she was. They called Thea, because the girl fit the description she'd given in her runaway report. When Thea got there, Elissa opened her eyes, so Thea seems to think Elissa knew she was there. But her injuries were too great; they couldn't save her."

Hannah's face crumpled and reddened, a sure sign that she wanted to cry but not in front of us. She swallowed hard and looked at RJ as though willing him to speak. RJ's blue eyes appeared enormous in his white face, but he glanced at his sister, and nodded.

"Kipling and Ralston? Was it that car accident we saw?"

I shook my head, feeling like I wanted to cry and knowing it was reflected on my face. "I don't know--it probably was the ambulance we saw. But it wasn't a car accident. Elissa was found in the field."

Hannah and RJ exchanged anguished glances. I hurt for them, hearing this.

"And they don't know who did this to her?" RJ's voice squeaked, something that hadn't happened in a while.

I shook my head. "The police are still investigating."

Pete stayed for dinner, but nobody felt like talking. And even RJ, who usually ate everything on the table plus whatever else I had in the house, picked at his food. It felt wrong somehow to be eating then. The kids eventually drifted downstairs to their rooms in the walkout basement.

I knew their questions weren't fully answered, but I doubted I would ever be able to answer them all. I felt inadequate. I collapsed onto the couch in the living room, staring numbly. Pete followed me into the room and watched me quietly, waiting for me to speak.

I ran a hand through my hair and shook my head. "I want to talk to you, but not tonight."

He came and stood over me, taking my hand to pull me out of the chair. We walked to the door.

"I understand. Tonight you have enough to cope with," Pete said lifting my chin with his finger so he could kiss me.

I watched numbly as he got in his car. The house stayed quiet. Doors closed, the shower went on and off, but neither one of the kids played their boom boxes. The rec room TV never flickered to life. I heard Hannah on the phone only once, and she cut it short.

I sat in the living room without any lights--wondering how it had been for Elissa--wondering how Thea would cope. Finally, unable to stand the quiet, and needing to know more, I snapped on the T.V., switching around some hospital drama and a news magazine until I came to the local news. Would there be anything about Elissa?

Hannah slipped into the room first. She'd changed into her plaid robe and slippers. After a glance at the screen, she curled up next to me, seeking some comfort.

As I stroked her hair, RJ drifted into the room. Like Hannah, he stood in the doorway, watching a moment. He wore the same black jeans he'd worn before, but his thick dark hair was weighted down with water and his chest was bare. He moved to my other side, eyes riveted to the screen. He sat on the edge of the couch, back straight.

I pulled him back against me, brushing my fingers through his hair, but he wouldn't relax against me. Did he know something more about Elissa? I'd thought yesterday he wasn't telling everything.

We waited dully through the national news, the screen bright in the darkened living room. It seemed an age before the handsome dark-haired newscaster said, "Finally an update to a story we brought you last night."

It was so silent in the house; it was as though not one of us even took a breath. "News Four has learned that the teenaged girl found in Arvada last night is dead. Indications are that the girl had been beaten. Her name has not yet been released and the matter is, of course, under police investigation. In other news tonight..."

I didn't want to hear any other news tonight. Pushing gently at the kids, I stood up and snapped the TV off.

Hannah fled the room, sobbing.

RJ looked at me blankly, eyes glittering with unshed tears before he too bolted from the room.

* * *

I didn't have to be up early since it was my turn to pull the night shift at work--a once a week rotation. I stayed up half the night, thinking and worrying and slept through the kids leaving for school.

Errands and cleaning took up the day but not my thoughts. I kept wondering if there was some way I could have helped Elissa. And what about my own kids? How could I help them deal with this? How could something like this happen? The idea of work would have been a relief if it didn't mean leaving the kids alone. My eyes felt heavy and my mind clogged.

The phone rang around two-thirty and I sprang to answer it, its noise an obscenity in the quiet. It was Pete, just calling to tell me he was there, if I needed him. Much as I appreciated the thought, I kept the call short.

Hoping for a quiet night, both at home and at work, I busied myself in the kitchen, making meatloaf for dinner.

The slam of the front door shook the house. "You know, it's not like you're perfect," RJ said.

"Shh, Mom's home, you idiot. Didn't you see the car?"

"Yes, Mom's home," I said, wiping my hands on a paper towel and walking out to the living room. "So what's up?"

Hannah shrugged, her blonde hair spilling out of her heart embroidered knit cap. "RJ's just being a jerk again." She moved past me to the stairway to her room, taking off her down jacket as she went.

RJ's eyes were narrow but he just shook his head at me.

Dinner started out quietly. The kids sat down as soon as I called, picking at the food without complaint. That should have been my first clue since meatloaf was no one's favorite dinner.

Hannah directed her small heart-shaped face at her plate and said oh, so casually, "Josh and I need to get together to study tonight."

"So you'll be going to the library? How will you get there?"

"No, we've got a pretty big math test. It's going to take a while." She glanced up, green eyes watchful. "I told him to come over about nine."

Nine. When I was due at work. I might be tired, but not out of my mind. "No boys in the house while I'm at work. House rules," I reminded her.

"Mother." Only a teenage girl could say the word that way. "You are treating me like a child."

"Hannah, I don't care how old you are. This is still my house, and I'm not going to let you have boys in here when I'm not home."

"Fine. I'll move back with Dad." She tossed her head, pushing her hair off her shoulders.

"You think your father will let you entertain your boyfriend in an empty house?" I stood up and scraped my plate into the garbage disposal. She'd soon find out that Roger was stricter on this one than I was. No matter what he'd done with that Bimbo he'd had the affair with, his daughter was definitely a different matter.

"I said we were going to study. It's not like a date or anything."

I shook my head, mouth tight, then spun on my heels and left the room to get ready for work. Hannah wouldn't drop it though. She trailed me, leaving her plate congealing on the table and staying on my case as I dressed. We argued right up until it was time for me to leave at eight thirty.

RJ watched silently, but I got the uneasy feeling he was satisfied about something. I walked out the door with no illusions that Hannah agreed with me. There wasn't much I could do about it, but hope that RJ would let me know if she didn't follow instructions. But despite their obvious disagreement--or maybe because of it, I wasn't even sure about that.

The kitchen of the Beginnings was empty, the sixty-watt bulb over the sink throwing shadows over the rounded top refrigerator and the long Formica-topped table. I shut the door carefully behind me and moved toward the light of the living room.

Bret, the red-haired counselor I was relieving, waved at me as I came through the kitchen doorway. She already had her jacket on.

"How's it going?" I asked.

"It's dead," she said. "I left the shift notes in the office."

"Good. I need a quiet night."

With another wave, she went out the door.

Martha, one of our older residents stood in the living room, dressed in a black wool coat and hat, putting on her gloves, apparently ready to follow

Bret out the front door. "I'm going to run down to the Seven-Eleven and get some pop," she said.

There was a giggle from the crowd in the living room.

What was that about? I wondered, running my eyes over the women sitting on the couches. No one said anything though. I nodded to Martha politely and turned toward the office. I heard the squeaking front door open.

It hit the wall with a crash. Anita stumbled over the bags she held in her hands and staggered in. She landed, dazed and on her knees, on the flowered carpet, her loose pants hiked up to expose white flabby legs. Her open coat revealed a rumpled red plaid shirt. Her hair slid out of her barrette and fluttered in the cold wind blowing in the open door behind her.

"I'm so sorry," gasped the older woman, holding her hands to her face and standing over Anita.

"You okay, Anita?" I stepped over and peered down at her.

She nodded sheepishly, her normally ruddy face even redder with embarrassment.

I smiled. "We've got to get that door fixed."

"It's not the door. It's my Mom. She's a klutz." The voice was loud and rude and could only belong to Anita's son Flynn, a kid we'd nicknamed the "teen-from-hell" when he stayed here with his mom. Sure enough, there he stood--a skinny five-foot-ten version of every mother's nightmare. He had a new haircut since I'd last seen him, shaved on one side and falling lankily to his shoulders on the other. His skin looked unnaturally white. His heavy wool coat covered everything else above his ankles except his army boots. And if I remembered right, he was only fifteen.

I turned my fascinated gaze away from him and winked and smiled at poor Martha, who had inadvertently opened the door to this. She nodded and backed out the door. I could almost hear her sigh of relief when she got it closed.

I wrinkled my nose at Flynn, to show him I'd heard his comment and didn't agree and offered Anita a hand up. "You sure you're okay?" I asked.

Standing, she examined her knees and hands then looked up at me to smile. "Except for my pride."

"You coming to talk to me?"

She shook her head. "To stay." Her faded blue eyes filled with tears, but I noticed her pale lips tighten with determination.

I gestured toward the office. With a small smile that didn't expose her teeth, she picked up the bags and walked in. Flynn stood there glaring and didn't even offer to help his mother. I saw Anita in and then shut the door carefully between us, surveyed Flynn, finger to my lips, letting the little twerp know I didn't like what I saw. I let the silence grow long.

He at least had the grace to blush but then again that could have been anger not shame. I wasn't inclined to give him the benefit of the doubt.

"You know, your Mom is going through a hard time right now."

He snorted. "She's the one making it hard. And you."

I raised my eyebrows, as much at his rude tone as at the statement.

His face reddened more and he exploded, "If you hadn't told her all that garbage about needing counseling, she and my dad..."

I shook my head and looked him straight in the eyes--which meant craning my neck up a ways. This little monster needed to have it laid on the line. I spoke softly but firmly. "I know this is hard on you. But I can't and won't permit your rudeness in this house. You will treat your mother with respect, and you will politely address each and every person you meet in this house."

To my surprise, he bit his lip, stared down at his feet and mumbled, "Sorry."

Not the most elegant apology I'd ever heard, but I'd take it. I nodded to the sofa, the one that clashed so hideously with the beige and rose flowered carpet. "You can sit there if you want. I'd like to talk to your mother alone." I let myself back into the office quietly.

Anita scrabbled for the tissues we kept on the scratched and dented gray steel desk, and quickly wiped her face. I pretended not to notice she'd been crying since that seemed to be the way she wanted it.

"Want to tell me about it?"

She hunched a shoulder. "There's not much to tell, except that you were right."

I carefully braced the wobbly desk chair with my foot and slid into it. It took talent. That chair had been the downfall, literally, of more than one counselor in this place. When I got settled, I said, "Did you confront your husband about the counseling?"

"Not at first." Anita shook her head. "Not yesterday at all. But tonight, Chuck came home drunk. He said he'd gotten fired, and it was my fault."

"Your fault he got fired?" Personal responsibility was not the hallmark of the average abusive spouse. Still I was curious as to how Chuck worked this one out.

"I told him we couldn't afford to buy a new Cadillac. He said it's important when you're selling insurance to look successful. Then you'll be successful."

That answered that question. I smiled sadly.

"But we didn't have the money," she burst out.

I nodded. "Of course, you said so. So what happened?"

"We sat down to dinner--the usual stuff. But Chuck kept yelling at me. 'Why did you make pot roast?' he said. I can't make pot roast--only his mother could. I couldn't do anything right. The place was a mess. He just kept going on and on. Pretty soon he just threw the plate--straight at me." Anita set her jaw, and sat staring stonily off into space.

"Did it hit you?"

She shook her head then reached for another tissue and blew her nose. "I ducked."

"Where was Flynn?"

"He sat there watching it all. He didn't say a word."

"What did you say when Chuck threw the plate?"

"I didn't say anything. Chuck didn't either for a minute--just stared at it. Then he told me to clean it up."

"Did you?"

"No." Anita shook her head for emphasis then lifted her chin. "I told him I wouldn't and that I wouldn't stay if he didn't clean it up. And when he got done with that, he'd better make an appointment for counseling."

"Good for you."

She shook her head again, mouth solemn. "No. That's when I should have left. He told me to." Anita's voice went up an octave. She swallowed hard, and used the damp tissue to mop under her eyes. "He said not to let the door hit me in the butt on the way out. But I didn't go. I was so mad."

Anita didn't seem the fighting type. What could she have done that she so badly regretted now? "What did you do?"

"I called his mother."

I couldn't help it. I laughed. Anita talked as though she'd done something terrible because she'd called his mother? I quickly sobered myself when I saw Anita's face.

She wasn't laughing.

"What did his mother say?"

"She told me to leave him. She said I didn't have to take this kind of stuff, and she hadn't raised Chuck to be this way. She left his dad because of abuse." Anita's face looked like a parody of the mask of tragedy. But it was obvious, she felt miserable, and I hurt for her.

"That's when I knew--even his mother was telling me--I knew you guys were right."

I couldn't ignore the huge tears streaming down her face now. I handed her the tissue box, and patted her hand. "I know that was hard," I said softly.

"I handed the phone to Chuck. He was furious. He kept asking me why I had to drag his mother into this." Anita sniffed. "I went into the bedroom to get some things together and go--and the whole time, I knew his mother was talking to him. And Chuck was yelling back. And I feel so--so..." She searched for the word.

"Upset?"

"Mean. I feel mean. Chuck was right. I shouldn't drag his Mom into it."

"You didn't do anything wrong, Anita. You just aren't hiding it anymore. Abusers thrive on keeping the abuse hidden. You've taken an important step."

Anita's blue eyes contrasted with her flushed face. "So why don't I feel better?"

I shook my head. Who could feel better in the middle of that?

* * *

When we came out to get Flynn and Anita settled in a room, we found Flynn sleeping on the sofa. Anita went to shake him awake.

The women who had been talking in the living room had moved to the opposite corner, whispering animatedly. Martha was back with her pop and at center stage. "...every single one of the shirts torn," she said.

The group laughed as though she'd said something uproariously funny. None of them noticed my approach.

"What's up?" I asked.

Silence fell heavy. Darla, the short, heavy brunette who'd been complaining to Dina about her roommate the other day, colored and stood up. "I'd better get to bed. I've got to be at work early," she stuttered. The other two women followed her, leaving Martha facing me.

"What's going on?" I repeated.

Martha gathered her big black purse and her pop. "Not much, Kaye," she said. "Just a little girl talk before bed." She smiled at me.

I let her go, but I resolved to keep my ears open a bit more. Something was going on, I knew it.

* * *

No one was up when Liz, my relief counselor, came in at 5:30. It had started to snow again and I felt glad to be heading home to my own quiet bed. All I had was a folding cot that I badly needed to replace. I'd been meaning to buy a bedroom set ever since I moved out of the house I'd shared with Roger. At first, finances made it impossible. Now that I had the money, there never seemed to be the time, which I regretted bitterly every night I slept on that cot. At that point I didn't care what it felt like though.

Or I wouldn't if it hadn't been for Hannah's boyfriend Josh. He and she were both in the front room, sleeping on the couch.

Chapter 5

But not for long.

I loomed over them glaring, sure they would wake from the force of my stare. When they didn't, I prodded first Hannah then Josh with my index finger. Hannah opened her eyes halfway and looked as though she were going to close them again. Josh stirred a bit, then opened his brown eyes wide, an uh-oh look on his face. He had that much sense; he knew trouble when he saw it.

"Out," I said softly.

Josh hastily disentangled himself from Hannah.

"Mom, for heaven's sake, it's not..."

"I said, OUT."

Hannah swung her legs to the floor and stood up. "Mother, you are treating me like a child."

I tightened my mouth and shook my head. Josh, all six stringy feet of him, at least knew enough not to argue with me. He put on his jacket, combed hastily through his brown hair with his fingers and left without a word.

Hannah was never that compliant or sensible. With her hands on her rumpled, jean-clad hips, she said, "Mom, this is jacked up. Just because you have to work, I shouldn't have anyone over? I don't think so."

I counted to ten. I had my father's Italian temper. The thought kept going through my head that she must have done this on purpose. I'd already told her how I felt. So maybe she wanted a reaction? I'd have to think about that. "We just got finished discussing this, Hannah. I told you--not in my house."

She twitched her blonde head at me irritably.

"We'll talk about this later," I said.

She breathed heavily out her nose. "I'm not a child, Mother!"

That was entirely the problem.

I shut my bedroom door behind me gently to let her know that I wanted this discussion over and that one of us had some emotional control. I wanted to let go of her gradually. In just a few years, she could legally make any kind of decision she wanted to. But not, I felt determined, in my house.

I took my clothes off and tossed them at the wicker basket in the closet that served as my hamper, arched my neck to try to relieve the tension, and lay down on that miserable cot. I had to get some sleep. Hannah could wait.

When I woke, the house felt quiet and cold. My windows were frosted on the edges, the blurry middles revealing a gray day with flurries dancing lightly in the air. I shivered and burrowed back under the covers. I turned the thermostat down while we slept or were away from the house. On these snowy days, it made it hard to get out of bed. I turned over and squinted at the clock I kept on top of clothes-filled boxes next to that cursed cot. Two o'clock. I'd better get up.

The kids would be home from school soon. I was hoping that RJ got home first. I needed to talk to him, and find out if his anger at Hannah had anything to do with her and Josh. I'd tried half-heartedly to broach the subject yesterday morning, but he had forgotten to set his alarm and didn't get up until six-fifteen. That gave him a scant twenty minutes before his bus to eat, dress, and gather his stuff. I did ask him if he got his backpack back from Zack's house. All I got for my efforts was, "Mom, I'm trying to get done here. I'm going to be late."

After I got done eating my breakfast and talking to him, maybe I'd be able to deal with Hannah. I stared blearily out the window as I ate a piece of toast and cream cheese. The snow that had been only an icy dusting when I went to bed, was a good six inches now. Predictably, the school bus was late, which made me antsy.

I glanced at the clock again. Maybe the bus wasn't late. Maybe both of them had stayed after school. But sitting there waiting at that table would only make me blue.

I set to work. Hannah came in at three, smiled coolly to let me know she was still angry, and went directly downstairs to her room. I decided to let her.

By 3:15, I had the kitchen clean, the bathroom straightened, one load of wash in the dryer and another in the washer. Hannah never left her room the whole time, the sound of her music the only clue that she'd come home. It didn't matter. I felt better. Some people I knew ate when they were upset, some people worked out. I cleaned. It didn't solve all my problems but at least I got to stew over them in a nice tidy house.

RJ came in whistling, but his face looked somber.

"Hey, where have you been?" I asked, coming up from the basement laundry to greet him. I could've bitten my tongue off immediately. I could have at least said hello. Fortunately, RJ didn't seem to notice. Or at least if he did, he didn't take offense.

He took off his coat, starting to throw it in a heap at the bottom of the hall closet, looked at me and reconsidered, hanging it carefully. "It's Friday, Mom. I have French club."

"Look, I need to talk to you about what's going on with you and Hannah."

"What makes you think I'm mad at Hannah?"

"That question, for one. I didn't say you were mad at Hannah."

RJ looked at me, sighed and folded up his legs to flop down on one of the floor cushions. There he sat propped against the wall, arms folded in front, staring at the wall across from him. "I don't want to talk about it, Mom. It's personal."

"Does it have anything to do with her and Josh?"

He shook his head and repeated, "It's personal, Mom. I told you." He got up and wandered into the kitchen.

That appeared to be all I was going to get out of him. I followed him into the kitchen where I found him leaning on the open refrigerator door as though mesmerized by the contents. I reached out to gently shut the door.

RJ reached into the refrigerator before the door closed and grabbed the leftover tortillas and the bowl of refried beans.

"Did you hear anything at school about Elissa's funeral?" I asked.

He shook his head. "They're not having one," he said, busily spreading the beans on a tortilla.

I got the feeling he needed to have something else to concentrate on, so he didn't have to look at me. I didn't need to see his face to know how sad he felt, his voice told me that.

"They have to have a funeral, RJ."

He shook his head, still not looking up. "Elissa's mom decided to · cremate her and take her back to..." he waved his hand as though the gesture would tell me where.

Oddly enough, it did remind me that Thea had originally moved here from someplace back East.

"New York?" I asked.

He shrugged, mouth half full of cold tortilla and beans. Swallowing, he said, "One of those places. I guess they'll have a service there. Anyway, some of the kids are meeting over at the field--to sort of pay their respects. I thought I'd go over."

I nodded slowly. It made sense. As a matter of fact, I wanted to go myself--to see the place where Elissa died. Hannah could wait. I grabbed my coat.

Predictably, RJ wasn't thrilled. At fourteen, it wasn't cool to be seen with mom. I understood, but right then, my own need drove me. So I compromised. I trailed a suitable three steps behind and tried to look like someone else's mother.

Snow fell in the tops of my boots, and bushes dragged at my coat. The wind stung my cheeks and ears. As we walked, other bundled figures streamed from the road, solemn and quiet.

Finally we reached a small, dark clearing surrounded by evergreens, not far from the street, where groups of kids stood, hugging each other and crying. I shivered. It felt so isolated. I heard the sound of cars as they zipped by the spot. But with the pine tree barrier and no houses or buildings near, the clearing was hidden. The wind whistled through the tree branches, somehow emphasizing the solitude. Yet Elissa had died literally just feet away from help. My heart ached at the thought.

I wasn't the only one who hurt. The field was covered with snow, notes, stuffed animals and flowers. As I watched, one girl lit a candle, and with a serious face, passed the light on. Soon a circle of crying kids held lighted candles they shielded from the wind with cupped hands. Elissa had a lot of friends.

I looked around soberly and decided not to go closer. Even though I'd known Elissa all her life, I felt as though I were intruding.

RJ nodded to a few people then glanced back at me as though to check out what I was doing. When he saw me hanging back, an exasperated expression crossed his face, only to be quickly replaced by sympathy when his eyes met mine. "Bunch of posers," he muttered, nodding at the crying kids. "Most of them didn't care jack about Elissa when she was here. Now they act like they were best friends." His face looked dark, and his mouth contorted with the effort to hold back tears.

Did he feel guilty that he hadn't been a better friend to Elissa? Was he wondering if he should have paid more attention to her on her last day? I needed to talk with him and make sure he wasn't taking too much responsibility on himself.

Two girls dressed in long black skirts and Egyptian looking eye makeup brushed by me, interrupting my thoughts. "Hey, RJ," said the short heavy one. She wore her hair buzzed on one side and long and lank on the other.

RJ didn't seem to find their apparel as strange as I did-- not even the huge staple the other girl wore in her nose. He simply nodded at them both, and came back toward me. I had to stop myself from staring. The girls walked up to a chalky-faced boy with impossibly black hair in a black coat, and the tall one hugged him, crying openly.

Omigawd. Flynn?

"What is he doing here?"

"Who?" RJ turned to see who I meant.

"That's Flynn Conners--Elissa's boyfriend. He's probably wondering what you're doing here," Hannah said.

I jumped. I'd never even heard her coming. Slowly I turned to confront my daughter's angry eyes. "So you decided to leave your room."

"I didn't know you were here," she said. She crossed her arms over her chest, a gesture complicated by her puffy pink down jacket.

The gesture irritated me, but I set my jaw hard. "We need to talk, Hannah. But even if we can't right now, I want you to remember who you're speaking to and what we're here for." My own voice sounded almost as cold as hers.

"What are you here for?"

I turned again to be confronted by yet another angry face. Flynn had come over to investigate.

"Hello, Flynn," I said coolly.

"What are you doing here?" he repeated.

RJ moved in front of me, smiling as though Flynn were someone really fascinating. "This is my mom," RJ said. "She knew Elissa."

I watched, horrified. Flynn was not someone I wanted my son to even know about, let alone like.

"So?" Flynn spat the word out, obviously unimpressed.

Like I cared. I wasn't on this earth to impress him. I would deal with him at work. My major concern at this point was my children. This kid was bad news, and I didn't want them around him.

"So she has as much right to be in this field as you."

Hannah? I turned around to make sure that I really did recognize the voice. Wasn't this the kid who wouldn't have come if she'd known I would be here?

She wedged herself between Flynn and RJ and glared right at RJ. "I want to go. I'm not going to put up with this jerk, just because he was with Elissa."

With Elissa? What did that mean? Did Hannah mean Elissa dated Flynn or he'd been there that day? Sometimes I thought the old terms were better--or at least clearer. I wasn't the only one to wonder.

RJ's face went slack with surprise, but he quickly covered it with impatience. "So leave." He shrugged, but his eyes wouldn't meet hers.

Hannah nodded, as though she'd just made up her mind about something. "Fine, if that's what you want," she said tersely to RJ. "Come on, Mom." She hooked her arm into mine and began to steer me away.

I couldn't take my eyes off RJ--or Flynn. I didn't want to leave my son there with that--that punk. Whether in response to my stare or to the implied threat in Hannah's words, RJ nodded at Flynn and reluctantly followed.

"Hannah, what is going on?" I whispered. "How do you and RJ know Flynn?"

Hannah raised her eyebrows, trying, I think, to look innocent. "He's just a kid from school."

I shook my head. "No, he is not. He doesn't even live in Arvada. He lives and goes to school in Denver."

That statement opened her eyes fast. "How do you know that?"

I pressed my mouth closed. 'Nuff said. I did have to protect client confidentiality.

Hannah smiled ruefully, shaking her head. "Elissa's mom must have told you. I heard she didn't like him."

I shrugged, neither admitting nor denying. The first rule in raising teenagers, as I'd learned long ago, was to stay one step ahead and never, ever to divulge any of the information sources that put me there. I threw a glance over my shoulder at RJ. He was still following--although his lower lip stuck out so far, he could trip over it. Just what I needed--a sulky kid.

"What did you just threaten RJ with?"

Hannah's face reverted to the blankly innocent. "I didn't threaten RJ."

I stopped and turned to face her, grabbing her by the shoulders and narrowing my eyes to let her know I meant business. "Yes, you did. What doesn't he want you to tell? How involved is he with Flynn?"

Hannah's face twisted. She looked at me, then turned and glanced behind us. I followed her gaze. RJ strode toward us. I couldn't quite decipher the look on his face. He looked anxious yet the lip still stubbornly protruded almost as though he was determined yet dreaded to hear what we were saying.

I hooked my arm through Hannah's and started walking again quickly, thinking hard. Hannah wanted to spill the beans, I could tell. But RJ had something on her that she didn't want known. What could it be?

Then it hit me. My God! I should have figured it out before. "Last night wasn't the first time Josh was over when I was gone, was it?"

Hannah's green eyes shifted around guiltily, an inane smile on her face. Bingo. The smile faded slowly as she obviously considered the consequences. Then with a sigh of relief, she nodded, not at me particularly--more a bow to the inevitable, I think. She started walking even faster, dragging me with her. "No."

"Hannah, I know that this seems innocent to you, but you're heading for trouble. I don't want you to end up pregnant. Don't bring Josh to the house when I'm not there."

"How do you know I'm not already?" she said, green eyes flicking toward me angrily.

"Pregnant?" I stumbled so hard I almost fell over. "This ground is so uneven," I mumbled. I grasped her arm hard and straightened myself.

"Of course, pregnant. Isn't that what you're worried about? How do you know I'm not?"

I thought rapidly, looking away from Hannah to the snow-covered field. Surely, she'd used tampons last month? I couldn't remember. "Are you?" I held my breath, but if she noticed she probably put it down to our breakneck pace.

"No." She finally stopped, and looked me full in the face. "It's not like that, Mom. Why don't you trust me?"

"Trust is not the issue, Hannah. It's testing human nature when two people who are..." I couldn't make myself say love each other although I knew that she believed that she loved Josh..."who are interested in each other spend too much time alone together. You are too young to be getting this involved. I mean it. No boys--nobody--in the house when I'm not home."

She shrugged, her eyes now focused on the ground.

"Is this what RJ is holding over you?"

"Yes." Her voice was low.

"Anything else?" As if that wasn't enough. My mother would never have let me live to see the sun rise if I'd had a boy spend the night even once.

She shook her head, holding it low so that all I could see was her long blond hair.

"And you knew about his hanging around with Flynn." It was not a question, obviously.

"Yes. I saw them together a couple of times over at the Rec center--and Flynn's called our house a lot." Her voice sounded even softer. "Everybody knows Flynn. But nobody likes him, and I told RJ that. He's messed up. I know I should have told you..."

"Never mind," I pulled on her arm to get her to look at me. When she glanced up, I smoothed her hair back from her face. "RJ is not your responsibility. He makes his own decisions--and you make yours. But from what I know of Flynn--he's involved with drugs. Just tell me, if you know, is RJ?"

Hannah gasped. "Mom, I'm sorry."

"Now what are you sorry about?" RJ, lower lip still prominent, had caught up with us.

Chapter 6

"RJ!" The tall girl with the nose ring ran across the field, her long black skirt trailing through the snow.

Her friend, the girl with the buzz cut, followed slowly, the pallor of her face emphasized by the heavy dark eye makeup they both wore. If I were her mother, I'd rush that child to the doctor, suspecting, at the very least, mono. Her coloring looked as pale as Flynn's. Now that I thought about it, that's probably where she caught the mono. If that's what it was.

RJ would find himself very soon at the doctor's. A drug screen would tell us what we were dealing with. I watched him turn and stride away to talk to the girls. Hannah, with a stricken glance at me, drifted over to the group.

Fine. I needed the time to get my thoughts in order. I wanted to decide how I'd deal with this. My first instincts were to grab RJ and shout into his face. "What's the matter with you? How could you do drugs?" My first instincts, I'd learned through hard experience, seldom turned out well.

I took a deep, steadying breath and absently watched my kids with their oddly dressed friends. All four kids' faces looked solemn. The girl with the nose bangle did most of the talking, gesturing animatedly.

With another calming breath, I waved at them and walked back toward the house. At the edge of our yard, I carefully skirted a smashed pumpkin left over from Halloween. I had to get a plan.

I felt sure my family doctor would administer drug tests without letting RJ know. We'd gone to this man forever. He and I had talked many a time about drugged out kids we'd come across. I knew he would want to help.

But first I'd call Roger and tell him what I'd learned. I owed him that. He'd been a lousy husband, but he loved these kids. Then I'd call the doctor. I wanted to know what we were dealing with. Maybe there was nothing to deal with.

Stopping at my back door, which led to the garden-level, utility room-- and from there to the kids' rooms, I squared my shoulders, searching through my coat pockets for my keys. Most teens did some experimenting. RJ was always the curious type. Maybe he'd just tried it out, then decided it wasn't for him.

Keys in hand, I stood motionless in front of the door, staring at it without really seeing it. I had to get myself together. I needed to be objective.

Deep breath. Okay, what about signs of drug use? I ticked them off on my fingers. First, the grades. RJ's grades were always up and down--but lately we'd been talking way down--one finger up. Then there were the mood swings. I put another finger up.

Of course, all teenagers had mood swings. It was one of the defining characteristics of the age. I wiggled my upturned fingers indecisively. And I'd never noticed red eyes or smelled marijuana around the house. But maybe we weren't talking marijuana.

I gave up on counting the signs of drug use, clenching my fingers into a fist instead. The problem was, all those signs were so ambiguous. I just didn't know. I shivered, only partly from the cold wind. Parents of teenage drug users exhibited some classic signs, too. Denial was one of them. I had to be careful. My strong desire to believe that everything was all right didn't mean it was.

Okay, so I wouldn't call Roger yet. There was nothing to tell really. First, I'd take RJ for a drug test--tell him he was due for a physical. He probably was. I'd always been up-front with my kids, but I had no problem being devious when the need arose. Right now I needed to search his room.

I glanced guiltily around to see the kids still at the edge of the field talking, then let myself into utility room. It would be just a short step down the hall to RJ's room.

The house smelled stuffy. The furnace hummed softly, and some rock music played softly. Hannah left the boom box on in her room again, probably.

I stepped down the tan carpeted hallway, not bothering with lights. RJ's room to the right looked dark and strewn with clothes--the usual mess. I kicked absently at the plaid boxers on the floor looking for bongs or matches.

Matches wouldn't necessarily mean anything though. He had incense. Oh, God. Maybe to cover the smell of... whatever? I dove feverishly through piles of dirty jeans trying to marshal my thoughts. I knew what to look for. I'd done an internship in a teen group home, and I'd seen it all. I just hoped I'd never see it at my home.

I took another deep breath. So far, I didn't see it at my home. The kid didn't have a mirror on the wall, let alone one to snort coke with. The piles of clothes concealed nothing more unusual then a bowl of soggy Captain Crunch in congealed milk. Disgusting but not hallucinogenic.

I turned my attention to the closet--empty except for a couple of comic books and some Mad magazines. That seemed logical since his clothes were slung all over the floor. The bureau? I was still fussing with a drawer when I heard the phone ringing. Now what?

I had no reason to be downstairs. The kids could come home any minute, and I'd have to explain. I dashed upstairs and grabbed the kitchen phone just seconds before it went to the answering machine.

"Kaye?" The voice belonged to Brenda, the mother of RJ's friend, Zack.

I reached behind me blindly for a kitchen chair, feeling a stab of disappointment. Stupid! I jeered at myself. Was I hoping for Pete? Never mind, I soothed myself. I'd see him the next day for our weekly breakfast date.

"Hey, how are you doing?" I asked, trying to make my voice sound normal. I could have saved myself the effort. Brenda didn't even notice.

"Rotten. No, make that miserable. How about fu... never mind. That's one thing I really haven't been for a while."

I stayed quiet trying to make some sense out of this. I heard the sound of her kids talking in the background.

Then she laughed shakily. "Can you meet me for coffee?"

"Right now? What's the matter?" I wanted to be supportive, but I needed to take in this information about RJ. Besides I had a couple things here I needed to get to. Like finishing my search of his room.

"I'd prefer to meet with you and tell you." Then in an impatient voice, she said, "No, Travis, I told you."

I heard some muffled sounds and then a loud bang as though she'd dropped the phone.

"Sorry." Her voice sounded louder now; this must be directed to me.

"It's okay. Kids always want to talk when you're on the phone," I said easily.

"You don't know the half of it. Listen, if we meet at Mickey D's, I can send the kids off to play."

"Zack won't want to play at McDonald's," I protested. He must be--what? Thirteen by now or pretty close anyway.

"Zack is staying home." If Brenda had sounded impatient before, now her voice was positively steely. "If he knows what's good for him."

I definitely would if I were him. She sounded mad.

"Kaye, I've got to talk to you." Her voice had changed again. She was practically begging. "Please."

Maybe she'd found evidence about drug use, too. Besides, what could I do? Feeling like a jerk for my reluctance, I said, "I'll be there."

To make myself feel as though I were at least doing something to solve my own problem, I put in a quick call to my doctor to see if I could squeeze RJ into his schedule the next day.

I was out of luck. They'd gone home for the day. I put down the phone and scratched out a note for RJ and Hannah and left.

* * *

I lived only two blocks from McDonald's, but still it was impossible not to speculate about the problem with Zack on the way. Was it in any way related to my problem with RJ? Before I even got parked, I caught sight of Brenda.

She was shepherding her two younger kids, Travis and Danielle, across the crowded parking lot. Danielle's long black hair was done in some elaborate loop, and topped with a bow. Travis was talking a mile a minute--which was pretty standard for most four-year-olds. Everything looked normal.

I waved, and Brenda looked up, her eyelids reddened and swollen. Then again, maybe not. She waved back at me, pointing me out to the kids, who waved dutifully.

I nodded and swooped down on a parking spot, right before some pimply-faced, teenaged jock in a new yellow Mustang got it.

All right! One for the adults. God, I was so sick of teenagers right then. All of them. If it wasn't drugs, it was sex or school problems. All they did was give their parents heartache. I got out of the car and did a victory dance.

The Mustang revved a little before going up the aisle in search of a new place. The kid saw me in the rear-view mirror and gave me the finger. I wrinkled my nose at him and grinned. Sore loser. Then I went inside to stand in line behind Brenda.

I tugged on Danielle's hair, and she turned around and giggled at me. "Hi," I said, pulling aside her coat so I could see what outfit she had on today.

That seven-year-old had a better wardrobe than most women I knew. That night proved to be no different. She wore a dress with a black and red pattern on a white background. The bow in her hair and her tights were both color coordinated with the outfit and chosen to warm her chocolate-colored skin tones. "That's adorable," I said.

"I picked it out," she said, looking up at her mom with a shy smile.

"I got a new shirt," said Travis, tugging at my sleeve, his large dark eyes anxious for my attention.

"Let me see, Bud," I said.

He smiled broadly, and unzipped his black nylon coat to display a red and blue striped shirt.

"That's cool," I said, smiling.

Brenda paid and hefted her tray, pointing with her chin toward a table near the playroom. "That okay?"

I nodded and stepped up to give my order. "Be there in a sec," I said over my shoulder to Brenda.

By the time I got to the table with my hamburger and fries, the kids had taken off their coats and shoes and left. The sandwiches at their empty places showed only one bite apiece taken out of them. Food couldn't begin to compete with the playroom.

I set my tray down across from Brenda. She slumped in her chair as though exhausted. I knew the feeling. "It's not drugs, is it?" I blurted out.

She widened her eyes, and her brows went way up. "You mean Zack? God, I hope not. The cops didn't mention that."

Chapter 7

"The cops?" I sputtered out the words. Oh, my God, this was worse than I thought. "I knew that Flynn Conners was no good. But how does Zack know him?"

"Flynn Conners?" Brenda first poked at her sandwich with a long red enameled fingernail, then she lifted off the top bun. Finally with the detached look of a scientist conducting an experiment, she set the bun top down, and shredded it.

"Never mind," I said hastily. "What's this all about?"

"Somebody over at the rec center saw the boys with Elissa the day she died. They said she left with them."

"Elissa." Boy, had I been on the wrong page. It seemed so long ago now, since I'd picked RJ up at the rec center, and met Thea searching for Elissa.

"RJ said he saw her," I said slowly. "But he said she left while they were working on their hook shots."

Brenda finally looked up from mangling her sandwich, her huge dark eyes shadowed. "Kaye, I don't know what happened, but these cops aren't fooling around. They wanted to know what Zack knew about her death. I'm scared."

So was I. First, I found out RJ had been hanging out with Flynn. Then Hannah told me about the drugs. Now this. This couldn't be. It just couldn't be happening.

* * *

"This is happening and you'd better pay attention. You need to hire a lawyer." Pete pulled the chair out for me in the little bakery-coffee house where we'd agreed to meet for breakfast the next day.

Sun streamed in the huge front window of the plant-lined restaurant. Indian summer had returned to Colorado, and I reveled in the warmth, almost managing to convince myself that yesterday's fears had been exaggerated by the cold gray weather. Still, I'd wanted to talk to Pete before I confronted RJ.

Now I wished I hadn't. What had I been hoping for?

I hooked the Shaker style chair away from the table with my foot and scrutinized it. Pete watched me, sandy brow furrowed.

Had I wanted him to tell me I had nothing to worry about? But he wouldn't, he was a practical man. As soon as he heard what Brenda said, it was obvious what his response would be.

My hands shook so badly I spilled the coffee in my mug onto the tray. My heart beat too fast and I just wanted to run. But I couldn't hide from this--much as I wanted to. So I stood in the sunny restaurant staring at the chair.

"Kaye, what is the big deal with the chair?" Pete asked. "Did you hear what I said?"

I wrinkled my nose, speaking softly. "I've been to this place before. They're none too careful with their table clearing--which you'd never guess by looking at their beautiful white tablecloths."

"You're checking to be sure they've cleaned up enough?" Pete's voice showed his disbelief.

I shrugged. It was pretty unbelievable.

"You're stalling," Pete said softly. "It's not going to help. You're going to have to face this and do something. I can help you."

Sometimes stalling was the last defense left. I chose to answer his chair question. "Last time, I sat in someone's leftover Napoleon. I've still got the stains on my good red skirt. No way I'm going to let that happen today." I gestured toward my peach wool jumpsuit.

Pete sighed heavily.

I avoided his eyes and set down the tray holding my coffee and sweet roll. "A lawyer for Zack?" I asked, scooting into the table and taking a cautious sip of my steaming coffee.

"A lawyer for RJ," he corrected. He plunked his own chair right in front of me, so I couldn't avoid looking at him without being pretty obvious. His gravely, professional voice was in complete contrast to his off-duty T-shirt and tight faded jeans. "I might know somebody who could take the case."

I put the coffee down abruptly, causing it to slop over the lip of the handmade, mug onto the tablecloth. It left an incriminating ring on the whiteness. "Why does RJ need a lawyer?"

Pete had taken his own sip of coffee, holding my eyes all the while. But he took a maddeningly long time to set down his cup. Framing his words perhaps?

"Kaye." He reached forward and held my hands. "You have to look at this from a police perspective. Why do you think the cops have talked to Zack and not RJ?"

"I don't know. Are you saying they're prejudiced?"

He shook his head slowly. "This isn't about Zack being black."

"Maybe they didn't get to RJ yet."

"Maybe." He said the word easily, but the skepticism underneath showed.

"You're saying that they haven't talked to RJ because they suspect that he's involved in Elissa's death?" My voice wasn't usually that high-pitched. I cleared my throat and swallowed in an attempt to bring it back to the right register. The next sentence came out as a whisper. "That can't be."

Pete shrugged, took his hands away from mine and picked up his ham and cheese croissant, took a huge bite, then shoved the food to the side of his mouth and talked around it. "You keep saying that. That's not like you."

"I hate that. I'm always yelling at my kids for that."

"What?"

"Talking with your mouth full. It's rude."

Pete's head jerked back in surprise. He swallowed, smiled tightly and said, "Now you're trying to change the subject."

"And the subject is that the police haven't talked to my son yet because he's a suspect in the murder of a girl he's known all his life." This time my voice came out right, if a bit cold--and loud. I felt the eyes of the people at the nearby tables on me.

"Kaye."

I didn't answer--preferring instead to turn my attention around the restaurant, letting my gaze drift around slowly and deliberately. Most of the other customers turned back to their own food--except for an overweight lady with stiffly styled gray hair at the table in back of Pete. Her eyes were fixed on us with no pretense of the polite deafness most people use in public.

I glared at her heavily. She smiled at me politely and I swear, leaned in closer to hear.

"She's not even embarrassed," I muttered, trying harder to glare her down.

Pete took my face in his hands and directed my gaze back toward him. When he knew he had my attention, he dropped his hands back to capture mine, holding them steadily, reassuringly.

"Kaye, you have to stop. We have to talk."

"You think RJ killed Elissa," I hissed. I looked down, trying to hold back my anger. This wasn't the place. But what was I doing dating a guy who thought my kid could kill? "What could there be to talk about?"

"I didn't say I thought RJ did it. I said, I'm afraid the Arvada police think he did."

I tried to pull my hands from his and leave. I didn't need to stay there and listen to him accuse my son. "And what evidence do you have to say that? They haven't even questioned him."

He held onto my struggling hands. "That's exactly the problem, Kaye. Cops try to interview anybody involved in a crime as soon as possible after the crime. But if they don't get to it right away, they might possibly wait to question someone who they see as a hostile witness until they have all their facts."

"Why would RJ be hostile?"

"The question is, why would the Arvada police think he's hostile?"

I settled my restless hands, but I wouldn't look up to see Pete's face. I didn't want to read the pity I felt sure was there. He was wrong. Couldn't he see that? "Okay, why? What do you know? Has someone told you something?"

"Kaye, this isn't my area, you know that."

"You didn't answer my question. Don't give me that it's not your area stuff. Just because you work as a Denver cop doesn't mean you can't talk to somebody in Arvada. What do you know?"

He put both of my hands in one of his and used the other to tilt my chin up, forcing me to look at him. It wasn't pity after all. It was fear I saw in his eyes. Pete Farrell was afraid for my kid.

"Someone has placed him at the scene already. They have reason to believe that RJ is involved."

That was pretty much what Brenda said. So why, when he said it, did my chest hurt? "I have to leave." I dragged my hands away from his and stood--reaching blindly behind me for my coat.

"What are you doing?" he asked. He stood up and ran his hand through his hair.

"Looking for my coat." I realized as I said it that I hadn't worn one. "I forgot. It felt warm this morning."

Pete smiled but his eyes crinkled down so the overall effect looked sad. "We need to talk about this, Kaye."

I shook my head--annoying tears blurring my vision. I couldn't even see if that snoopy old lady was still listening in. I glared in her direction just in case. "I've got to get to work."

He nodded.

It was only in the car on my way into Denver that I finally asked myself why I was crying. I often cried when I was angry. But obviously I had no reason to be angry. How could I be mad at Pete for worrying about my son? I wasn't that unreasonable. I squinted into the windshield, my tears glittering rainbows in the gorgeous Indian summer sun. Was I upset at RJ? That question dried my eyes--a good thing because I had to get to work.

* * *

The crowd of on-lookers was back at Beginnings. Martha, an older woman who was quiet enough with the counselors but who always seemed to have enough to say to other residents, was at the center of women standing at the front window of the Safe house. Of course, Darla, her short heavy figure clad in a sweater that clung too tightly, was there, too, along with a couple of other women who were new to the shelter. All of the women were visibly craning their necks looking at the restaurant/lounge across the street. All of them were grinning.

I turned to see what they were all looking at. The restaurant's parking lot seemed to be full and traffic trawled the small lot looking for parking spaces. But at the far corner of the lot, there was a gray-bearded man dressed in an expensive looking, black overcoat and charcoal slacks standing next to a blue Mercedes with what appeared to be four flat tires. He kicked one disconsolately.

"What the heck?" I said.

Darla snickered.

"The poor guy," I said.

One of the women snorted. "Yeah, right, the poor guy."

A horrible suspicion crossed my mind. I narrowed my eyes looking from face to face.

Martha looked back at me innocently. "After all the trouble we've all had with men, Kaye, you can hardly expect us to be sorry for any trouble any man has."

I said slowly, "I don't expect you to stand in the window applauding their problems either."

Darla and Martha looked at each other. The other two women, glancing warily at me, were already melting toward the back of the house.

The man across the street took no notice of us, walking toward the restaurant with his cell phone to his ear, his bearded chin bobbing animatedly as he spoke.

Martha shrugged and smiled at Darla, who couldn't seem to suppress a giggle. Then without a word, they both turned toward the kitchen.

I had no time to think about the incident. I had my own problems to confront again when I got the women dispersed.

Flynn perched sullenly in the white rocking chair, his face echoing his black T-shirt and jeans. Did he ever go to school?

Someone sat on the couch reading the Rocky Mountain News. From the glimpse I got of faded strawberry hair and homely brown dress, I guessed it was Anita. Then the front-page headline caught my eye--'Teen Battered to Death?'

"Hey," I said weakly, eyes glued to her paper.

"Hi, Kaye." Anita lowered the paper and peered over it. "I was reading about that poor girl in Arvada. Have you heard about her? They seem to think it was drug related."

Abruptly, I was angry again, but this time I knew the cause. "Really?" I turned toward Flynn, teeth barred. "She was a friend of yours, wasn't she?"

Anita's eyes flicked rapidly toward her son. It didn't appear as though she had known that.

Flynn's eyebrows drew together ominously but he said only, "I knew her, yeah." He emphasized knew.

I decided I'd scored enough there. "Actually," I looked at Anita, "so did I. I lived next door to her family for years."

"Oh, Kaye, I'm so sorry." Anita flushed and I knew she was worried that she'd made a terrible social blunder by bringing the subject up.

I waved away her apology. "It's her mother I'm sorry for. This is really hard on her."

Flynn snorted. "Oh, yeah," he muttered.

I raised an eyebrow. "You think that's funny?"

He shifted in his chair to sit up straight and glare. "I think she didn't care jack about Elissa. All her mom wanted was for Elissa to look like a good little girl. Just so it looked good to the neighbors."

"I consider Elissa's mother a friend, and I'd appreciate it if you kept those kind of opinions to yourself."

Flynn shrugged. "Whatever. If you can't take the truth."

"Whatever," I echoed coldly. I turned away from him deliberately, directing my comment to his mother. "I can't imagine that this thing is drug related though."

Flynn's voice challenged me. "Are you saying that you had no idea that she did drugs?"

I looked back at him, confronting his dark eyes with my own. "I knew she had a problem with drugs, yes. As a matter of fact, despite what you're trying to say about Elissa's mother wanting to keep up a front, she was the one who told me. Are you saying Elissa was involved with the kind of violent back-alley gangs who would beat her to death?"

The silence in the room crackled with electricity. I felt a calming sense of satisfaction. Let him get himself out of that one if he could. After all, he'd admitted knowing Elissa.

Flynn got the message. His eyes flickered fire.

His mother's eyes ping-ponged back and forth between us, her brow lowered in confusion.

"Actually," Flynn drawled. "I don't think it was some gang at all, according to the paper there." He pointed to the news in his mother's lap. "They found a backpack by her body, with some books spilling out. And some of the books were bloody. They're speculating that whoever killed her, started hitting her with the books. And finished her off with a rock. Most gangs I've heard of use guns--knives--fists, not backpacks."

Chapter 8

Abackpack? RJ's backpack? My God. This was what Pete had known and wouldn't tell me. But what did Flynn know about it? Did he know RJ's backpack was missing? That was a question I'd save for later.

"Kaye?" Anita's voice sounded concerned. "Are you okay?"

"I'm fine," I lied, smiling mechanically. "Got to get to work."

"Maybe you ought to go home," Flynn said.

Anita glanced at her son, her face shining with pride. I supposed it did sound thoughtful. But I knew better. Flynn was implying I should go home and talk to my son. I was dying to do it, too, but he'd gone to school already--unlike Flynn.

Check and checkmate for Flynn.

"Got to get to work," I repeated. I turned away blindly and stumbled into the office, closing the door behind me.

My boss, Liz Winfield, looked up from her desk, and ran a small square hand through her hair. "You okay?" she asked, eyes narrowed in concern.

"Traffic," I said.

"Oh, I know." She turned back to the papers on the desk. "The mousetrap is impossible since half of California moved here, and the road construction is even worse, isn't it?"

I grunted agreement. "Why isn't Flynn in school?"

"Anita was worried that his father would pick Flynn up at school, so we arranged with the district for him to do his work here for a while. There's not a problem, is there?"

Nothing I wanted to discuss with my boss, much as I loved her. Roger and Pete, I would discuss it with. Oh, God, and RJ himself, of course. But not Liz.

With an effort, I decided to change the subject to something I could discuss with her. "No. No problem at all. I need to talk to you about Martha. Or maybe Darla."

Liz raised an eyebrow.

I perched on the corner of the desk. "I don't know what's going on for sure, because neither of them are my residents, but I've twice come on the two of them laughing rather nastily about something, and then shutting up when they notice me. I'm getting the feeling one of them is... maybe stalking her husband?"

Liz looked thoughtful. "Darla's one of my residents but frankly, she doesn't strike me as having the guts to stalk."

"Maybe stalking isn't the right word. But maybe some kind of revenge? Do you have any idea what her husband looks like? There was an older man in the parking lot of the restaurant across the street with four flat tires. I hate to accuse anyone but Martha and Darla seemed to take a lot of enjoyment from the sight."

"Humph--an older man? It doesn't sound likely to be Darla's husband..."

The ringing crisis line cut off our discussion, but I had no worries. Now that Liz was alerted, the problem was as good as solved and I could use the free part of my brain thinking about my own fears. The morning passed in a blur.

While Liz went to lunch, I managed to put a call through to Roger. Naturally, given the time, I got his secretary.

"Mary, it's Kaye. I've got to talk to Roger."

"Can I have him call you back?" Her voice was sympathetic. She'd always liked me--even after the divorce. "He's got a meeting."

Roger was notorious for late starts--so much so that my family had named a whole time zone for him. There was real time and then there was R.A. time (Roger Atchinson time) where all times were adjusted by one hour. So if someone said, "I'll be there at noon R.A. time," they really meant they'd be there at one. That being the case, I had a good suspicion what was going on now. "C'mon, it's lunch time. What did he do--get there late and run over?"

Mary laughed. "That's about it."

"But I really need to talk to him. Couldn't you interrupt him for one brief second?"

Mary was quiet. I could almost hear her considering.

In a low voice, I said, "It's really important. He'd want to know."

"Okay." Her voice sounded decisive. "Hang on a minute while I transfer you."

I took a breath while I tried to plan what I would say.

"This is Roger."

The sound of his deep voice threw my plans out the window. I forgot that this man had cheated on me; the divorce hadn't been as amicable as it could have been and after all that, he'd had the nerve to ask me to come back to him. I remembered only that this was the father of my son, and RJ needed him.

"Roger, you've got to come over tonight, and help me talk to RJ. Elissa's dead and the police think he did it. And between what Hannah told me about the drugs and now this business with the backpack, I'm worried sick."

I thought the line was dead; his silence went on so long. Finally, he said cautiously, "Kaye?"

"Yes, Roger. It's me. Did you hear what I said? Did you know about Elissa?" He should. He still lived next door to the family. The kids and I were the ones to move out to a smaller house.

"I'd heard about the incident, yes. It's been all over the news. I sent Thea and George a sympathy card."

I supposed he meant he'd had Mary send a sympathy card. Still his guarded, not to say stuffy, response reminded me he was in a meeting. I tried to choose my words carefully.

"Roger, RJ and a friend of his were seen with Elissa shortly before she died. The police have already questioned his friend. Now it appears Elissa was beaten with a backpack full of books and RJ's backpack is missing."

"Kaye, you sound hysterical." Roger didn't bother to keep his distaste from his voice. "Do you realize what you are accusing him of?"

"Did you see the paper this morning?"

"Which one?"

"The Rocky. For God's sake, Roger, it's probably in the Post, too."

"What is in the paper?"

"The business about the backpack." How long would it take him to get this? Why couldn't he understand?

"This makes no sense at all." His voice sounded impatient. "Can I call you back?"

"No!" Later this office would be crowded with women and their counselors. I wasn't ready to deal with this at work either. "Roger," I strove to make my voice calm. "Go read the paper. Keep in mind that RJ was seen with Elissa that afternoon, and his backpack has been missing ever since that day. Then come see us tonight. And bring Art."

"He's not that kind of attorney." Roger's voice implied I should have known that, since Art was, after all, a friend. But since Art had represented Roger in the divorce action, we hadn't been exactly close lately.

"Ask him to recommend someone then. But bring him." I hung up and put my head in my hands. Then straightening my shoulders, I picked up the phone again. I dialed the number of Pete's cell phone, something I would not normally do during working hours-his or mine. He picked up on the first ring. Lucky me. Too bad for him.

"Why didn't you tell me you knew the Arvada police had RJ's backpack?" I was not exactly showcasing my phone manners today. Not that I cared.

"Kaye?"

"You got it." I felt angry, and yet I fought off the urge to cry at the same time. Consequently my voice sounded like someone with an extremely sore throat talking through clenched teeth.

"You want to have lunch?"

He sounded so calm, so sensible, so dependable. Naturally, I broke down and bawled.

"Honey, I'm sorry," he said after a minute. "I'll pick you up--and we'll go somewhere quiet where we can talk. Hang on."

I nodded stupidly into the phone, tears dripping down my cheeks. My nose ran almost as fast.

"Kaye? You're all right?"

"Yes," I sniveled.

"You still at work?"

"Uh huh."

"Just wait right there. I'm coming."

"Okay." I sniffed.

It was a stupid thing to agree to. I couldn't leave the safehouse until the other counselors came back from lunch. If he got here before they did, I was stuck. I did have the sense to powder my nose so when I could leave, I could do it without looking too much like I was one of my own clients. Then I paced the office as time crawled.

Things shook out better than I could have predicted though. Liz came back just as Pete pulled his pickup into the parking lot, so my explanations were kept to a minimum.

The brilliant sunlight made my eyes squint after the relative darkness of the safehouse. I collapsed into the passenger side and pushed a brown bag to the middle of the seat. Without a word of greeting to him, I slammed the door shut.

He started the truck with a grunt, and pulled out of the parking lot, gravel flying. "So the Arvada police have got RJ's backpack?"

"They've got a backpack. The paper doesn't say whose it is. But RJ's is missing." Now that I'd stopped crying, I was definitely back in the clenched teeth stage, and my voice reflected it.

"So you haven't heard from anybody. This is all from the paper?" he asked.

I nodded.

"That's good."

I didn't see anything good about it. It wasn't what he said this morning either. He was the one who told me I should be worried that the police hadn't talked to RJ yet. He couldn't get around me with meaningless garbage now.

"You're pretty mad, huh?" he said, looking at me sideways.

I nodded emphatically.

"I didn't know for sure what the Arvada police had to link RJ to the crime. I just knew they had some evidence."

"You did talk to someone about him!" So much for his "not-my-area" argument this morning.

He hunched a shoulder and looked straight at the road, which was crowded with the late lunch hour set. "I have a friend there; someone I went through college with. We both worked campus security. He ended up on the force in Arvada, me in Denver. So, yeah, I called him up. Asked him about the Pappas case. When he asked me what my interest was, I said I had a friend who was interested, meaning you." He shifted his gaze with a brief nod toward me then turned back toward the traffic. "Never mentioned any names though."

Pete turned the wheel, turning onto a quiet tree lined side street. He slowed down as we got to a small park. Velvety green grass sprinkled with fallen leaves advertised the warmth of the sun. But yesterday's snow still clung stubbornly to the ground in the shady areas. Pete maneuvered the truck into a small sunny slot on the swing set side and shut the engine off. "The thing is he and I have kept up pretty well, over the years. He knew I was seeing you. He asked me if you were the friend. When I said yes, he told me he couldn't tell me anything."

Pete picked up the paper bag that I'd moved when I got in the car and extracted a huge sub and a couple of cans of 7-Up. The paper crackled as he unwrapped the sandwich and split it. He offered me half.

I stared at the sandwich in his hand. I'd been so angry-- thinking he knew something I didn't. Now I didn't know what to think. The aroma of onions, pickles and vinegar filled the air, reminding me I was hungry. Still, something was missing from this story.

"That was it? He didn't tell you anything?"

Pete's blue eyes met mine. "He didn't have to tell me anything then. Just the fact that he wouldn't say anything, meant that you--or more probably, given what I knew--RJ was connected somehow to this crime."

That was so dumb it bothered me to think I understood it. "You knew because he wouldn't tell you? That makes no sense."

"If it didn't have anything to do with you, he would have told me anything I wanted to know. But since he couldn't tell me anything, you had to be involved." He nudged the sandwich toward me.

I turned in the seat and looked him squarely. I wanted to see every expression--every thought that passed over his face. "It sounded to me like you knew this all along. When we talked this morning, you kept telling me to get a lawyer for RJ."

He curled his mouth into a tight-lipped smile. His eyes stayed wide and serious. It was one of the saddest smiles I've ever seen. "As I said, I knew something was up. I still think you should get RJ a lawyer."

I nodded and sighed, taking the sandwich he still held patiently for me. "I got that. I'm working on it."

I left work early, complaining of a headache. Actually, I hoped to give RJ one. I'd decided to be there to talk to him when he got home from school. I even left the car a block away where he wouldn't see it on his way from the bus. Just so I could have the advantage of surprise.

The surprise was on me. I might as well have parked right in the driveway. The cops did.

Chapter 9

Two policemen were just sitting in their cruiser, waiting. I debated turning around on the street, getting in my car and catching RJ as soon as he got off the bus. I could take him to his Dad and get a lawyer. I shook my head slowly. Maybe RJ didn't even need a lawyer. I needed to find out what the cops wanted.

I walked slowly up my cracked driveway, my gray flats scuffing at the fallen brown leaves. I kept my eyes ahead on the uniformed policeman, who got out of his car as he saw me coming up the drive. The other, older cop, dressed in gray Dockers and a polo type shirt, followed more leisurely.

"How's it going?" Tall, blond and young, the cop nodded at me, as though he were my host.

"Officer, what can I do for you?" I asked. I smiled but my heart was pounding.

"Mom!" Hannah must have been watching for me. She stood in the doorway, barefooted. "They want to talk to RJ."

I nodded coolly, keeping my eyes on the cops the same way I would keep my eye on dangerous snakes which were about to strike. "He's not home yet, is he?"

"No. Dad's coming over," Hannah volunteered.

That made me shift my eyes to her. I lifted my eyebrows in question.

"I called him when I couldn't get you," she said. She pointed at the plain-clothes policeman. "He said he needed to talk to a parent."

The police couldn't question a minor without a parent. I knew that much from accompanying clients to these kinds of interviews. My heart hammered so fast now, I felt sure it skipped a couple of beats. I made an effort to breathe deep and concentrate. "What are you doing home?"

"Dad said to tell you he's bringing Art," Hannah said, ignoring my question.

I nodded, making the effort to stretch my mouth up to form at least a straight line. I acted as though this information was very much a matter of fact for me, instead of the subject of debate that it had been earlier in the day. Hopefully Hannah had been able to get her father up to speed on the situation better than I had. "What are you doing home?" I repeated. "RJ usually gets out first."

"My gym teacher never showed up," she said, looking at the cops.

I frowned. Something was wrong with that answer, even if it was hardly the point at the moment.

"Excuse me for saying so," said the older cop, turning my attention back to him. "But you don't seem very surprised to see us, Mrs. Atchinson."

"Berreano," I corrected automatically. "I'm divorced from RJ's father."

I shrugged my shoulders, when I felt more like shivering--not for the first time that day. Whatever had made me feel like it was warm this morning? This Denver sunshine and blue sky was deceptive. Either that or Indian summer was a lot colder than it used to be. "I understand that you talked to Zack Washburn the other day. This is about Elissa Pappas, isn't it?"

"That's right," said the blonde, easily. "I'm Officer Tom Quarters and this is Detective Deaton. We're investigating the Pappas case. We have a few questions that we'd like to ask your son."

Officer Quarters couldn't be Pete's friend. He looked too young to have gone to college with Pete thirty years ago. He looked too young to have been born thirty years ago.

Maybe that was what was the matter with me. It wasn't cold. I was getting old. "Would you like to come in?"

Hannah's eyes widened.

What was I supposed to do? I couldn't leave these guys out here to let the neighbors see the whole thing.

"Actually," Officer Quarters hesitated, then appeared to change his mind about what he had been about to say and leaned back against his car. "Is RJ due back soon?"

"There he is now." Hannah pointed down the street.

RJ's tall, skinny figure moved slowly up the hill. A black backpack, which I recognized as last year's model, dangled by one strap. His army style coat was slung carelessly over an oversized shirt; his jeans inched down past his boxers. Only his dark hair looked neat and cared for. That was probably because except for the top, it was shaved.

At the same time, a shiny, new, blue Mercedes drove up and beeped at RJ. Roger had arrived, driving his newest toy--the one designed to make me regret that I'd not only divorced him but that I'd fought him for the Volvo. All I cared about at the moment was whether he brought Art with him. RJ needed a lawyer.

A power red Jaguar ripped around the corner in answer to my unspoken question. Art, too, was recently divorced. Frankly, my sympathies went to his ex, Cynthia. But I liked his car. Right about then, I would have liked a Pinto if that was what he wanted to drive. The cavalry had arrived.

I sagged in relief, turning back to explain to Officer Quarters, who was still propped against his car. "That's RJ's father in the blue car."

"And the red car behind him is his lawyer's," exulted Hannah.

Slowly, both cars pulled up to the curb. Roger got out of the car, picking nonexistent lint from his dark blue suit as he strode up the walk.

Art smoothed the wisp that covered his bald spot, buttoned his suit coat and gathered up a black portfolio. Then he stood fussing with some buttons on his car.

Roger extended his hand, his face smiling and confident. "Officer, Roger Atchinson." He introduced himself. "What can we do for you today?"

Officer Quarters pushed himself off his car. "Mr. Atchinson." He nodded affably and extracted a card from his pocket and put it in Roger's outstretched hand. "I'm Officer Quarters." He nodded at his partner. "This is Detective Deaton. As I believe your daughter must have told you on the phone, we came to talk to your son."

Deaton scowled at Roger. Could he really be Pete's friend? He didn't look very friendly to me.

Roger studied the card he'd been handed, and then flipped it casually toward Art who had just sauntered up the drive.

Art palmed the card, glanced at it quickly and inserted it smoothly into his portfolio. "Officers." He nodded. "I'm Arthur Patterson. I represent the Atchinsons. I understand this is about the Pappas girl."

How did Art do that? In one small sentence--really one phrase--he made Elissa sound--unclean. Like she was the problem not the victim.

Did Art know the Pappas? I couldn't remember. It was possible that back when I was doing the wonderful wife and hostess thing, we'd had a party where both the Pattersons and the Pappas were invited. So they could be acquainted. Not that it mattered.

RJ finally ambled up to the house then, and ignoring the adult confab in the driveway, headed for the front door. How could he? Didn't he know what this was all about? Even if he didn't, wasn't he curious? Cops didn't come to our door every day.

I summoned my voice. "RJ, could you come here?"

My call coincided with Roger's. "Yo, RJ."

I glared at Roger. It was my house. I stepped forward toward RJ. "These gentlemen..." with a sweep of my arm, I indicated the policemen..."came here to speak with you."

If I was looking for some reaction from RJ, I was disappointed. His face was not just blank, it was dull as though my son had vacated the premises and left a mannequin in his place. What was he on? I hadn't been able to get him to the doctors for the drug test yet. Now I regretted that bitterly.

Officer Quarters handed RJ a card.

How many of those did he have?

"I'm Officer Quarters, RJ." His voice was gentle. "I'm here to talk to you about Elissa Pappas."

"My mom just said that," RJ said. "So talk."

"Actually, I would like to take you down to the station, where we can get your statement on record."

Art coughed and moved forward. "Certainly, officer, we want to do everything in our power to help your investigation." Art put his arm around RJ.

RJ hunched his shoulders and glanced at Art from the corners of his eyes. I wondered if RJ felt as uncomfortable as he looked since he stood a couple of inches taller than Art.

"We can meet you down at the station house," Art said.

Quarters kept his face carefully professional as his eyes met his partner's. He nodded agreement. Maybe it was because he was so young, the polished professional facade wasn't quite as tight as it could be. Anyway I could tell that things weren't exactly the way he wanted.

"Okay, meet you in the front lobby in ten minutes," he said.

There would be no time to regroup. It took almost that long to get to the police station.

Quarters and Deaton got in their car and drove off, all of us watching. Then as if a signal had been given, Art, arm still around RJ, and Roger started toward their cars. As if in afterthought, Roger turned around and smiled at me. "Kaye, don't worry. We'll take care of this."

Was he trying to tell me not to come? Even he couldn't be that dense. God, he was a jerk. I bit my lip and counted to ten, not saying anything to him. It was so fifties--the little woman attitude. I blew a deep breath out. Typical Roger. But I had to remember RJ needed us both right now. I smiled, gritting my teeth. "No bother. Of course, I want to come."

RJ got in the car with Art--presumably so he could give RJ some counsel on the way to the police station. Roger got in his car, smiling his huge fake smile at me.

I ignored him and turned to Hannah. "Don't worry, honey."

"When will you be back?"

I shrugged. "It depends on how long this all takes. I don't know. But I better get going." I started back down the drive.

"Mom, where's your car?"

"I left it down the street." I called over my shoulder. Then feeling sheepish, I turned around and walked backwards so I could face her. I didn't want to explain about how I had planned on surprising RJ. Besides, given her answer about school, I might need this technique to catch her cutting class. "I needed a walk." I finally explained lamely.

Her eyebrows flew up, but she didn't say anything, so I waved, and turned back around. I had to get going. It took a couple of minutes to get to the Police Department, and I didn't want them to start without me.

The lobby of the police department was nothing more than a large tiled room with a few orange and blue plastic chairs lining the walls around it. Doors led off from it in all directions. On one side was a telephone, next to a large glass window. A large sign above the window said Records. Beyond the window, several women worked behind desks in what looked to be a typical clerical office.

I took it all in quickly. I'd been here before. Part of my job was to be a victim advocate. Many times, clients called right after their husbands had beaten them, so of course we counseled them to call the police. Often, we accompanied them to the police station to make a report.

I'd never come to the police department for my personal life before. Somehow, that made it all look different.

RJ slouched in one on the plastic chairs. Art and Roger stood over him, talking desultorily. Deaton came through a door on the left, just as I stepped up to the men. That door I knew. It led to the hallway outside the interrogation rooms. I saw no sign of the friendly and readable Officer Quarters.

Deaton jerked his head at us and said, "If you would all come back here, please."

He led us down the narrow, institutionally carpeted hall, past the rooms I knew. Finally he stopped in front of a solid looking door.

"Before we go in," he said, looking at RJ. "I'd like to make sure that you are carrying no weapons."

RJ's lip curled. "Like I would."

Deaton lifted an eyebrow, and cocked his head to include Art in the discussion. "Just routine procedure."

Art nodded, although nothing about Deaton's manner made me think he'd been asking permission. My heart, which had calmed its aerobics somewhat during the driveway exchange, started up again.

"Could you put your arms at your side, please." Deaton stepped forward as he spoke.

RJ took his hands out of his pockets in response, and stood rolling his eyes as the cop quickly patted him down. The search yielded nothing more interesting than RJ's doodled on but otherwise blank notepad and a rubber eyeball at the end of a long elastic band.

Deaton studied the notepad a bit before handing it back silently. Then he took a key off his belt and opened a door, holding it for us. "It's going to be a bit of a squeeze," he said.

He wasn't kidding. We had to crowd in. Then we stood in a clump, just looking around the room.

Even the institutional carpeting ended at this room's doorway. Shining white linoleum covered the floor and a bare table stood against the wall. The white walls completed the picture of a cold barren place. Above the table and on the opposite side of the room were dark mirrors. I knew that someone stood on the other side of those mirrors, watching. If the sight of Deaton frisking my son hadn't clued me in to the gravity of this interrogation, this room would have told me. It fairly shouted the news. This was serious stuff.

Detective Deaton came in back of us and sat down, motioning for us to do likewise. There were four chairs crammed along the table so tightly that no space came between them. RJ sat first, with me next to him and Art on his other side. Roger opted to stand in back of RJ.

"First of all," Deaton said, "let's get the obvious out of the way. What does RJ stand for?"

There was a short silence then Art and I answered him together. "Roger Junior."

RJ himself stayed silent. Flustered, I glanced quickly at Art who smiled at me. Then I shifted my gaze back toward Roger. He put his index finger to his lips and jerked his head to Art. I felt a stab of irritation, quickly replaced by compunction. I had asked for Art to be here.

Meanwhile, Deaton had written his information down and moved on. "I need to talk to you, RJ, about November tenth. Do you remember that day?"

RJ glanced at Art, who nodded encouragingly. Then with more than a bit of sarcastic bite to his voice, RJ answered, "Duh, November tenth. I wonder." His voice became sharper and louder as he scowled into Deaton's face. "Like it's every day that somebody I've known all my life gets killed. Of course, I remember."

If he had just been a kid I knew, like Flynn, the voice alone would have been enough to make me want to shake RJ. As it was, since he was mine, I wanted to hide my face in embarrassment. I really had raised him to be more polite.

Deaton betrayed neither emotion. His face stayed professionally blank, his voice courteous. "You want to tell me about that day?"

"What do you want to know?" RJ shrugged, and looked uncertainly at Art, who nodded again.

"Were you at the rec center that afternoon?" Deaton asked.

RJ relaxed. Art had apparently okayed this line of questioning. "Yes. Me and Zack went there after school to play basketball."

"Did you see Elissa?" Deaton asked.

RJ's gaze flew to Art's face. I don't know what he saw there. Art looked pretty blank to me. But RJ nodded and stared off into space as he spoke. "Yeah, we saw Elissa. I talked to her a few minutes and then I went back to my game. End of story." He glanced at Art as if to say, Okay, I did what you said then looked back at Deaton.

"Is it?" asked Deaton softly. "Didn't you leave your game and take Elissa over to the field off Kipling?"

Just what was he trying to imply? I strained forward. "No!" I said fiercely. "RJ wasn't at the field at all. I know. I picked him up at the rec center that day."

RJ turned pale and swallowed, glancing again at Art, who appeared as though he'd just made up his mind about something. He shook his head at RJ.

"I think you should know, RJ," Deaton said softly. "We have evidence linking you to the scene."

"Yeah, right," RJ bit out. "You don't have jack."

In that same soft voice that seemed so menacing, Deaton said, "We've got your backpack."

Although I'd had all day to get used to that idea, it still struck me hard. I held my breath, and kept my eyes so firmly on RJ they felt stuck open. RJ's emotions passed over his face like shadows. His eyes flew open, and his whole body jerked back. He looked... surprised. I was in turn surprised myself. Was he the only one in the room who didn't know? Then his shoulders sagged, and his mouth tightened. I wouldn't say he looked relieved. It was different from that. It was almost as though he just grasped some unwelcome fact.

Finally RJ looked at me from up under his lashes and then back again at Deaton. "Yeah, me and Zack walked her over to the field, because she was supposed to meet somebody there."

I gasped. Did RJ know what he was saying? What he was admitting to? I'd asked him this the night Elissa went missing. Was it all a lie?

"But we came right back. I got friends that will swear to that." RJ added hastily.

"I'm sure you do," said Deaton.

His voice flowed smoothly and affably, but I had no doubt he implied that RJ and anyone who would be friends with RJ would be willing to lie. I felt frozen now, but the sweat started to flow under my arms. My hands shook so much that I had to hold them tightly clasped in my lap.

Art scooted his chair back and started to say something, obviously ready to end the interview. RJ waved him back, abruptly. Even though I knew it probably wasn't in his best legal interests, I felt glad. I needed to hear what RJ had to say.

"I loaned the backpack to a friend of mine," he said carefully. "But when I asked him about it, he said he'd given it to Elissa to give to me."

"So did she?" Deaton asked.

RJ shook his head in a quick firm denial. "No. She didn't have it that day."

Deaton raised his eyebrows. "Who did you lend it to? Was it Zack?"

"No," RJ shot back. "I don't think it matters who I loaned it to. He isn't involved in this."

"Then how do you explain how it got there?"

"I don't know."

"So Elissa didn't have it. You didn't have it. No one else was at the scene with you but Zack Washburn and he didn't have it. But somehow, this backpack ended up at the place where Elissa was killed. Somehow this backpack just happened to end up with your friend Elissa's blood on it."

Art stood up. "Officer, we've been willing to cooperate with your investigation," he said. "But I really cannot allow you to badger my client."

"Are you willing to allow your client to give us hair and blood samples?" asked Deaton.

"No," said Art. He bent to speak to Roger behind a shielding hand.

"Yes," said RJ. He stood up so abruptly, his chair fell over with a screech and a clatter. He ignored it and faced Art, jaw jutting, eyes narrowed and sparking with anger. "I didn't hurt Elissa. I would never hurt her. They can have hair samples, blood samples. I'll do a lie detector test. Whatever. I don't care." He swung around toward Deaton, the movement wild almost--savage.

I looked at RJ wondering if I even recognized this child. When had he changed from my happy-go-lucky kid to this? Did he hurt Elissa? He looked fierce enough--scary enough.

RJ drew his eyebrows into one straight line across his forehead, his face distorted with anger. "I didn't do it, and I want you to find out who did."

He paused as if to see Deaton's reaction. He might as well have kept going. Deaton's face stayed blank.

RJ formed his words with exaggerated slowness. "And when you do find him, he better watch out."

Chapter 10

Art whispered fast and furiously to Roger. It wasn't addressed to me but that didn't mean I couldn't hear it, despite Art's hand held up in front. As his parents, Roger and I could object to the hair and blood samples. After all, RJ was a minor.

Roger kept his face calm, but he ran a hand through his hair, a gesture that served to tell me exactly how upset he was. Roger never allowed anything to muss his hair. His eyes met mine over Art's head. Then he cocked his head toward me in question. After twenty years of marriage, I knew what he was asking.

Should we object? I shook my head no, slowly.

The corner of Roger's mouth turned down, wryly, but he nodded agreement. We were together on this one. We needed to know, one way or the other. We wouldn't object.

Art threw his hands up in frustration.

Deaton gave us a slew of papers to sign. Releases for the medical information. Then he brought the backpack in, encased in a plastic bag. No touching. Deaton turned it around several times for us to inspect.

I was surprised at how innocuous it looked. It was only a plain dark blue backpack with a leather bottom. I'd expected to be repulsed by this thing that had hurt a child I'd known. Surely, she hadn't really been killed by it.

Still, I'd expected it to be gory with blood. The bloodstain, if that's what it was, was a tiny brown spot on the bottom. The sole identifying factor, really, was RJ's rendition of the grim reaper done in typewriter eraser fluid on the back side, but it was enough. Everyone identified the backpack as RJ's.

More papers to sign.

And all the time, we waited for an Emergency Medical Technician to come and take the samples. Deaton left us for what seemed like forever alone in the cold bare room. Nobody talked. We sat and waited.

I watched RJ dully. My throat ached from my need to cry. I kept sniffing it back. All I could think was, this is my kid. Nightmares shouldn't be so real. We should be talking about his report card and our plans for Thanksgiving. Instead... I couldn't finish the thought. I ached some more.

By the time the EMT did come, I felt so tired, it didn't matter that they took RJ into the jail to get the samples. The technician sat RJ at a one-armed desk reminiscent of a school child's. Art, Roger and I stood around awkwardly and watched the blood flow into the tubes. With a snip of the scissors, the hair sample was taken and finally we could go.

Yet even after our long wait, it seemed incredible that it could be after eleven when we finally walked out to the parking lot. The air felt cold, but the clear sky sparkled with stars. I looked up and couldn't believe the world looked so normal. It wasn't right.

Art fell into step beside me, leaving Roger with RJ. "You should get some dinner, Kaye," he said. "You look beat."

I shrugged. "I'm not hungry." I looked up at him. Art wasn't all that tall, but then, I was pretty short. "I appreciate you coming here with us tonight, Art."

"It's not my field." He smiled and shook his head. "And RJ didn't listen to the little I do know about it. I'm not sure I did you much good."

I put my hand on his arm. "Still, I appreciate it."

Roger and RJ caught up to us. I felt awkward and tense-- then I thought--screw it. There were bigger things in life to concentrate on than my divorce from Roger.

Roger looked sideways at my hand on Art's arm but he said simply, "I'm going to take RJ out to dinner, Kaye. You want to come?"

I shook my head. At that point, food would have choked me. I couldn't believe Roger wanted to eat. RJ, of course, was always hungry, but it would be late by the time they got done. Not that it mattered to Roger or RJ. Tomorrow was Saturday. RJ and Hannah usually spent Saturday with Roger while I worked. "He can stay at your house tonight, if you want." I could use the time to think.

For the second time that night, RJ jerked back, almost as though he'd been hit. Had he wanted to come home?

"That okay?" I asked him.

He shrugged.

I shook my head at him, and grabbed his arm to kiss him. "Get some sleep. We'll talk tomorrow."

Roger nodded as though I'd been talking to him. RJ didn't react at all.

"Okay." Roger cleared his throat, glanced quickly at Art, then at me. "Well, goodnight then."

I nodded, smiled at Art and moved quickly to my car. It was cold and I needed to go home and rest.

* * *

Hannah couldn't have known what kind of night I'd had, but really after our last fight she could have at least gotten Josh out of there before I got home.

Maybe she just wasn't a devious kid. More likely she thought that this police interview thing would leave me too shaken to object. I did admire guts, but not in my living room at eleven o'clock at night in direct disobedience to what I'd told her only days before.

I slammed the front door hard enough to make the two of them sit up on the sofa--a feat in itself considering that they were so intertwined. And to think I'd been glad to get the furniture in the divorce. I should have stuck with throw pillows and the bare wooden floor. Then there would have been no soft, comfy sofa to make out on.

The breeze raised by the door ruffled Josh's fine brown hair, which already stood in an electrically charged halo around his head. He brushed at it as though at a pesky insect and peered at me anxiously.

Hannah's shirt was bunched up showing her stomach. She saw me looking at it, and smoothed her shirt down self-consciously over her jean-clad hips. She licked her lips and shifted her weight from one hip to the other.

I couldn't decide whether she felt nervous or was smart enough to know she'd better keep quiet while she marshaled her arguments. I smiled wickedly and turned the overhead light on. The better to see them both with.

"Josh, I think you'd better go home." I said it calmly, but my children would recognize it as a dangerous calm. Josh had no idea what he had gotten into.

"No, Kaye, I have to stay with this. This was my idea, too."

I was probably old-fashioned or stuffy as Hannah frequently called me, and I knew I was definitely out of fashion, but I did not like my children's friends calling me by my given name. I believed if they spoke to me with respect, they were more apt to give me respect. I was aware however that this was no longer common practice. Not that that stopped me. "Call me Ms. Berreano," I said sweetly.

Hannah rolled her eyes, but Josh, to do him credit, merely nodded. "Okay. Ms. Berreano, I think that I should be a part of this discussion, too."

"Fine." I gritted out through my teeth, just before the phone rang.

I was inclined to ignore it. After all, who in the name of all that was wonderful would call at this hour of the night that I wanted to talk to anyway? Hannah must have been glad for the interruption. She picked up the receiver. Wouldn't you know it? It was Roger. Thrills. What happened to dinner? They could barely have gotten through a fast-food drive-through in this amount of time. Still that was always RJ's favorite source of nourishment.

"Tell your father that we are in the middle of something. This is not a time to chat."

Hannah put her hand over the mouthpiece. "He called to talk to you about RJ. Where is RJ anyway?"

About time she asked. RJ could have been arrested for all she knew. "He's staying with your father. Tell Roger I'll talk to him tomorrow."

Hannah looked sidelong at me. I knew she was considering how she could draw out the phone call. Now that she had the attention she wanted, it suddenly didn't look so great. But one look at me told her it wouldn't get any better either. She spoke into the phone, "Dad, Mom says she'll call you tomorrow."

Suddenly, I had a better idea. "Why don't you tell your father exactly what's going on here?" I'd chipped a tooth talking with my jaw clenched that way before, but it kept me from yelling when I was that angry. And the other person still gets the idea that maybe I wasn't too delighted with them right then.

Hannah looked at me with startled eyes, wanting me to know that she didn't want him to know about this one. I widened my eyes right back at her, wagging my head. She was his kid, too. Her mouth tightened, and she flipped her hair off her shoulder. Then she deliberately turned away from the sight of me, and spoke into the mouthpiece.

"Mom's ticked because Josh stayed over here with me tonight."

I punched the speaker button on the phone, so Roger could get the full gist of the conversation. "After I told you that I was not going to have him in while I am not in the house."

Hannah reluctantly set the receiver down. Having the call open to all was not what she wanted.

"Ms. Berreano, I know that this is hard for you to accept, but it is a new century now, and Hannah is an adult," Josh said.

"Not in my house," roared Roger.

"My house," I chipped in.

"She's still my daughter, too, you know," Roger said.

Hannah turned to me as though waiting to see how I'd take that.

Actually, I had no quarrel with that, as long as he argued my way. I turned to Josh to finish that argument. "Just turned fifteen is not an adult."

"Still you have to understand that things have changed since you were our age and..."

"Where do you get off telling me it's okay for you to mess around with my daughter because it's a new century?" It was amazing how loud someone could be over that speakerphone. I'd have turned down the volume if I could do it without the kids seeing.

"Surely, Mr. Berreano..." Josh mumbled.

"Atchinson," Roger roared again. "And I don't want some snot-nosed teenager in there diddling my daughter and then telling me, I'd better get with it, it's a new century. I don't care if it's the year twenty-five twenty five."

"Dad!" Hannah sounded appalled.

I wondered if it was Roger's yelling at her boyfriend or his phraseology that offended her.

"Go to your room, Hannah," he bellowed.

Turning down the volume on the phone probably wouldn't help. I needed to have a volume switch on Roger. His throat must surely have ached. It was hard to keep yelling like that.

"He can't do that." Hannah looked at me as though expecting me to save her. "This isn't even his house."

"Allow me." I bowed to the phone, smiling grittily as though Roger could see. Then turning to Hannah, I said, "Go to your room, Hannah."

"Mother!"

"Now."

"You are both treating me like a child." She scanned my face and then apparently not finding an opening there, she spun around and stomped out. Seconds later, I heard the slamming the door of her room.

"I think you'd better go," I said to Josh.

"But, Ms. Berreano..."

"Now," Roger roared again.

Luckily the kid was pretty speedy. The door was no sooner closed than I collapsed on the floor laughing, although I tried hard to do it silently so Hannah couldn't hear me.

"Do you want to tell me what you think is so blasted funny about that?" Roger asked.

Better to keep this to ourselves. I stood up and punched the speaker button again, and picked up the handset. "Everything." I managed wiping tears off my cheeks. "You and I cooperating, which I'll tell you, Hannah never expected, their faces, the whole miserable thing."

"Our daughter is sleeping with some little pimply faced jerk, and you think that's funny?"

"Well, let's just say it's easy to see where she's getting this from."

It was a low blow, and I knew it. Yes, Roger had been having an affair at the time of the divorce, but that had been over for months. He'd even asked me to come back. So where had that outburst come from?

"Great. Just great, Kaye. Is that how they taught you to counsel people? Lay on the blame. But while you're at it, start at home. Why didn't you stay home tonight? I told you Art and I could handle it. Some supervision is what she needs."

"Fine, Roger, so are you volunteering?"

"You got that straight, my dear. You've got both of these kids so screwed up, I'm not sure I can straighten them out. But I'll try. I'm volunteering," he stressed the word, "for custody."

I struggled upright for the parting shot. "You already tried that one, dear." I emphasized the word to show what I thought of him calling me that. "But by all means, take me back to court. The results were so good the last time."

The slamming down of his phone in my ear was his answer.

Hannah stalked back into the room.

"Way to go, Mother. The only time in months that you guys agree on anything, and you have to blow it. You really don't want to get back with him, do you?"

I didn't know that Roger had discussed this with Hannah. He'd asked me months ago--but I'd given him my answer. "What is it you want me to say, Hannah? No, I don't."

"Well, you might consider me and RJ. We didn't want you to get divorced in the first place. Doesn't that count for something? You don't seem to want this guy you've been dating either."

I raised my eyebrows. No way was I discussing Pete with Hannah.

The fact that she had raised no response from me didn't stop her. Oh, no, not my daughter.

"And this place..." she gestured around the living room, "sucks."

That stung. True, this house wasn't in the same class as the one Roger owned, but it was a good house in a decent neighborhood. Not only that but it was the best I could do. I was more tired now than I'd been in months and it was suddenly too much to argue. "Go back to your room, Hannah."

"No." Hannah also had a dangerous but quiet tone.

I waited for her to tell me she was going to move in with Josh. What she actually said was easier to take.

"I'm going to stay with Dina."

Dina lived about two miles away. She and Hannah had become best buds since Hannah started baby-sitting for Dina last year. I could deal with that.

"Maybe, Mother, when you can treat me like an adult, I'll be back."

Was Dina still up? When did she have to work tomorrow? I wasn't sure. Sometimes it was hard enough to keep up with my own schedule, let alone my co-workers'. Still I had to agree Hannah and I would benefit from the breathing space and there were worse places for Hannah to run to.

As I stood deliberating, Hannah rushed downstairs where I heard her hurriedly shutting drawers and rummaging around. A few moments later she stomped back up, clutching a bulging black backpack. It looked like she was going. And I was going to let her. Buses were still running that way. And the bus stop was just up the street where I could keep her in sight until she got on.

I hoped it was okay with Dina. After Hannah tramped out to the bus stop, I decided to call and find out. Gaze riveted on Hannah as she waited for the bus, I dialed the cordless.

"What are you doing still up?" said Dina's sleepy voice.

I must have woken her. That thought gave me a pang of remorse. I remembered what it was like to get up in the wee hours with a little one. I bit my lip. "Listen. I need to talk to you. Hannah's on her way to your house."

Dina took the cue and made her voice upbeat in response. "You really wanted to be sure that I got up, huh?"

"Yeah."

"Had a fight?"

"A humdinger. Even Roger got into this one, and then after we dealt with her, we fought with each other."

"Good one!"

"Yeah, so do you think you could meet the bus and maybe keep her tonight? Let's see. This is Friday. She goes to her Dad's house tomorrow. Maybe it will all blow over if we have a break from each other."

"You going to tell me what this is about?"

"Oh, sorry. I thought I did. Boys, of course. Her sex life."

"Lock her up until she's twenty-one."

"Yeah. Roger almost did tonight."

"Ooh, I'll bet. His little girl."

"Don't say anything to her, Dina."

"I won't. She'd never tell me anything again. But you're making me glad this one I've got is a boy."

"That's no guarantee you'll understand him better," I said thinking of RJ.

"Thanks for the encouragement," said Dina.

"Anytime. But you'll keep my kid?"

"No problem. Phil's been pulling a lot of overtime, it will be nice to have the company."

Dina's husband Phil had recently taken a job as a reporter for a radio station. I wondered how that was working out, but I didn't ask. I couldn't take any more right then. I heard the sound of the baby crying.

"Oops, got to go. Talk to you later."

"Yeah. Dina?"

"What?"

"Thanks."

"Anytime."

I hung up the phone and stared around my empty living room, listening to my empty house. I'd thought I'd gone numb. But my sobs filled the empty space.

Chapter 11

Tiny white Christmas lights twinkled on the store windows of Old town Arvada as I drove home from work the next evening. Clumps of people roamed the streets, swaddled in coats and holiday smiles. Evergreens decorated the lampposts and snow fell softly, melting on the streets as it hit. The tires of the car made a swishing sound as the car radio played "*Let it Snow*". It was my first "holiday" song of the season and should have completed the holiday feel. It didn't.

Yellow light poured out of houses in nearby streets into the darkening night and made me feel lost and alone. The thought of Thanksgiving--not much more than a week away, overwhelmed me. It would be the first holiday season since my divorce. The first one since my niece Mo, who we normally got together with, went back East to live. The first one alone with the kids--if I had the kids.

Maybe Roger was right. Maybe this was my fault. I'd tried to do right by the kids, but maybe it wasn't enough. I'd changed my work schedule when I got divorced so I would be home with them at night. It still wouldn't pass the Dr. Laura test. I wasn't home with them when they got home from school. But I used to work every night. Now I only worked one night a week.

But there was never enough time. Not at work, not at home with the kids, certainly not with the chores. The house was always a mess, the fridge always empty.

I straightened my aching shoulders, a difficult task in my bulky coat. I heard and felt my neck crack. As I did, I spotted movement out of the corner of my eye. I was just passing Lawrence Elementary. The handsome brick building was shrouded in darkness except for the lobby lights.

But in front of the darkened playground, stood a big seventies-something Buick with a Sesame Street paint job. There couldn't be two cars like that in the whole Metro area. Flynn had to be around somewhere. Not that it was any of my business. The safehouse required Anita to be in by six for house meals and meetings, but her son had no such limits. So I really had no reason to care why he was there. Just call me curious.

I slowed the car and craned my neck as I passed. I saw a couple of shadows in the farthest corner. Assuming one was Flynn, who was the other one? I could barely make out the outline of the figures--it was so dark.

I slowed the car to a stop, shutting off my lights so I wouldn't be seen. Scooting over to the other side of the car, I pressed my nose up to the cold window. I knew I'd make a print on the window that I'd have to clean the next day. It didn't matter. All I wanted to know was who was with Flynn and what were they doing.

Stopping had done nothing to improve the view. I cursed under my breath. If I really wanted to know, I'd have to get out. I pushed the button of the overhead dome so the light wouldn't give me away, eased the door of the Volvo open, and slid off the seat. Then I pushed the door almost closed. I didn't want the click of the latch to betray me.

A sudden spurt of traffic along the road in back of me masked my footsteps' noise on the gravel. I dove for the shadows of the climbing fort, keeping my eyes on the pair the whole time.

As I did, I thought something changed hands between the two. A bag of something. Alarm bells went off in my head. I couldn't be witnessing what I thought I was witnessing. But what else would make Flynn meet someone in the shadows of the evening on an empty playground? If I needed confirmation of my drug fears, there it was. The murmur of their voices was too faint for me to make out any words--or identify the other speaker. Then, with a wave of his hand, Flynn started to move toward me. The other one caught him by his black over-coat, causing Flynn to turn around. Lucky for me.

That was when I realized the trouble I'd be in if Flynn caught me spying on him. I scrambled back across the gravel, out of the playground, keys in hand and slid back across the driver seat and turned the key clumsily. Out of breath, my hands shook as though I were the one doing something wrong. The shift lever felt stiff and cold under my hand. I kept the lights off and inched the car forward, still looking at the playground.

Flynn's face was a white blur coming toward me, but his familiar lope confirmed his identity to me. I strained my eyes to find his buddy. The shadows behind Flynn moved and solidified. As he passed under the streetlight, I recognized the tall stringy figure of Hannah's boyfriend, Josh. In his white and purple Arvada West High School jacket, he was unmistakable. I swung the car into gear and took off, my thoughts in a whirl. If Josh were into drugs, could Hannah be far behind?

* * *

The house was dark when I got home, only a faint flickering behind the living room curtain betraying a presence. RJ liked to watch TV in the dark. Roger must have dropped the kids off right on schedule at six. I consulted my watch. It was only a few minutes after. At least the kids had probably eaten. They always ate dinner with Roger on Saturdays. The rumblings in my stomach weren't all due to my nervousness about what I'd seen.

I took a deep breath and inserted my key in the dark keyhole, trusting to the feel to make sure I'd inserted the right key. I needed to get a security light or something that would flicker on when it sensed movement. Then I wouldn't be stuck out on the darkened front stoop because my kids had forgotten to turn the outside lights on for me.

The door stuck a little so I kneed it. It flew open and banged against the wall behind it. Instinctively, my hand came up and flicked on the overhead light. RJ hurriedly straightened up on the couch and blinked. His hair looked a bit mussed, his oversize jeans and long-sleeved shirt hung in wrinkled folds around him.

I must have woken him up. "Sorry," I said, pulling the door closed behind me to minimize the chill. "I didn't mean to startle you." I tugged off my coat and hung it in the tiny closet behind the door, sniffing. What was that smell? I turned to examine the room for a clue but saw nothing. The TV set blared making me turn that way. Football--must be some college team. Another of his endless sports programs.

"Where's your sister? Did she go to your Dad's with you?"

RJ blinked again and shrugged. "She was there. She said she would stay with Dad this week," he said slowly.

When I turned my eyes on him, he blinked yet again, and licked his lips. Finally he offered, "Dad said she had to call you and make sure it was all right. But she said no. So he said she better come home."

I looked around the living room empty except for us, hoping for some clue. She wasn't there. She hadn't been with Josh. "Where is she?"

He hunched his shoulder and looked away from me, his eyes red rimmed. The butterflies in my stomach were fluttering stronger. It was obvious Hannah wasn't here. And even more obvious that I'd interrupted

RJ in the middle of smoking something. It couldn't be candles, could it? The smell was strangely sweet.

"When we got here, she filled up her backpack and left. Said she was going back to Dina's."

I nodded and turned to the stairs, blundering loudly down the wooden steps. I snapped on the light in Hannah's room. I don't know why. I knew he'd told me the truth. She was gone. And it wasn't likely I'd be able to tell what she took with her either. Knee high piles of clothes, liberally peppered with the occasional CD, filled the floor. The comforter hung half off the bed. Rap music played from the stereo. But the room was empty.

I lunged over the clothes, hoping I wouldn't land on anything breakable and switched off the radio. I would call Dina later and make sure Hannah was there. RJ was my priority now, I decided. With another leap, I left the room, shutting the door behind me.

With a guilty glance upstairs, I headed down the hall toward RJ's room, sniffing as I went. It got colder the closer I got, and the sweetish smell hung heavier in the air. His room looked dark and pretty much as it had when I saw it last. Which is to say, a mess to match Hannah's. I sniffed some more and shook my head. What was that smell? Incense? I moved to the center of the room, but it still didn't help. I couldn't tell.

But at least then I knew why it was so cold down there. He had his window open. In the middle of a November snowstorm. Why? To rid the house of that smell? I carefully maneuvered through the debris on his floor and pulled the crank on the casement. As I did, I noticed a strange looking glass pipe full of ashes in the snow collecting outside. What was in that? God, I wished Pete were here. As if in answer to my thoughts, someone knocked on the upstairs door. I practically ran out of RJ's room and took the stairs two at a time. I needn't have bothered. A glance in the living room showed RJ asleep on the couch. The door reverberated to the beating it was getting. He didn't stir.

I shook my head and headed into the darkened kitchen. I wasn't going to open it up. It was probably one of his friends. Besides, I didn't feel like talking to anyone right then. I needed food and some time to think.

But Brenda's voice, muffled by my closed front door, stopped me with the refrigerator door half open, its light spilling out into the room. "Kaye, please. If you're in there, please, I need to talk to you."

Suddenly I wanted to talk to her as badly as it sounded like she wanted to talk to me. Were Zack and RJ doing dope together? What was going on? I sprang for the door, and pulled it shut behind me, with one cautious eye on RJ. Brenda, herself, surprised me. No hat, no gloves, no coat--despite the snow fluttering down on us. She was dressed as impeccably as usual in a fluffy pink sweater and grey wool pants, but she hunched her shoulders against the cold.

I gestured toward the house, against my better judgment. There would be no way to have the private conversation I was hoping for in there. But I didn't want her to freeze out here either. Not to mention the fact that I hadn't exactly come running out the door with my own coat on either.

But she shook her head vehemently. "Oh, God! Kaye!"

"Hey, what's going on? Are you okay?"

"I'm not sure," she said so quietly, I had a hard time hearing her

Her eyes were aimed at our feet. Then looking up, she wailed, "Why did you let RJ give his blood?"

Whatever I had expected, it wasn't that. I hadn't told anyone that RJ had given blood samples to the cop. Not Hannah, not Dina, certainly not my boss. No one but Pete. "Slow down a minute. What are you talking about?"

"Detective Deaton brought Zack back in for questionin'. He said he'd questioned RJ and RJ gave blood and hair samples and they matched!"

That wasn't possible. I wasn't up on forensic pathology, but I was pretty sure that no one could do genetic testing in one day. "What did they match?"

Suddenly the overhead light flickered on and the door, which I had been leaning on, moved away from me. If I hadn't already had my hand to my mouth, I would have screamed.

RJ stood in the doorway, eyes blinking, his dark hair sticking upright. He held an almost full ice cream carton in his hands, a spoon stuck directly in the carton.

Sometimes I wondered why I even bothered to own dishware.

"Hey. What's going on?" he asked sleepily.

"What do you mean? You startled me, that's all."

He smiled and said, "So, what's happening?" He took a huge spoonful of ice cream and popped it in his mouth.

I opened my mouth to admonish him, but what was the use? It wasn't likely there would be any ice cream left when he was done anyway. Besides, I had bigger worries with this kid than ice cream. I needed to talk to Brenda.

"Brenda stopped by to talk to me a minute."

He nodded, still smiling, mouth still full of ice cream. "Later," he said, waving his spoon at Brenda. Then he retreated back inside, the door latching loudly behind him.

Whispering loudly, I moved closer to Brenda. "What did RJ's hair and blood match?"

"Deaton said they did a type and cross, whatever that is, and they matched the blood type on the backpack."

Oh. It was possible to have done blood typing on RJ's blood in one day, and cross-matched to the blood on the backpack. It would be a faster way to rule someone out. But hold it-- wouldn't it be Elissa's blood on the backpack?

"Kaye?"

"I'm still here. Did Deaton say anything else?"

Slowly she shook her head. But she said, "He just said it'd go better for Zack if he admitted to the crime before they charged him for it. He asked

Zack for hair samples and stuff. I told Zack we're not doin' nothin'--not even one more word until we get a lawyer." Her voice grew emphatic on the last sentence.

"You don't have a lawyer yet?"

"No, that's why I'm here--to ask you who yours is. Deaton told me," her voice broke. "That it would be better if Zack and RJ had different lawyers. He sounded like he was only bein' nice when he said it--but that just made it harder."

"Yeah, I can see how it would," I said glumly. Obviously, this was not the time to talk about the kids' drug habits.

Chapter 12

I closed the door and stood staring out its diamond shaped window into my dark front yard. Brenda drove slowly away, headlights picking out the snowflakes ahead of her. From the kitchen, I heard the clatter of pans. RJ had the munchies.

Pete had been right the other day. I couldn't hide from this thing--it wasn't going away. It was only getting worse. I needed to deal with RJ.

I tapped my fingernails thoughtfully on the door and moved across the room to pick up the phone. Then abruptly, I set it down, and moved into my bedroom to pick up the cordless. I needed a closed door between RJ and me. It was time to sit down and calmly discuss all this with Roger. He had a right to be in on this.

"Roger?"

"What's wrong?"

Okay, so my voice wasn't as calm as I'd hoped. I took a deep breath and sat on the edge of the cot. I tried to speak softly so my son wouldn't overhear. "Everything! We need to talk."

"Kaye, I thought we handled the incident yesterday pretty well."

"Oh, you did? Roger, there's more than you know going on here. RJ's blood matched the blood on the backpack, he's been doing drugs in his spare time, and Hannah is so angry at me she's staying over at Dina's."

I must have been a fool to blurt all that out to the man who had threatened to take me back to court for custody just the night before. It was on the tip of my tongue to tell him about seeing Josh with Flynn on the playground, but for some reason I didn't. God knows why since I didn't bother to restrain myself with any of the other problems.

"Roger?"

I heard a big sigh.

"Kaye, I was going to tell you that you needed to get a grip, but I did that the other day in my office. And you weren't as hysterical as I thought."

He was listening at least. I heaved out a breath of relief. Then I waited-- for what I wasn't sure. This sounded like the opening to an apology but I hadn't had many of those in all the years we'd been married.

Finally he said, "Peace?"

"Peace," I agreed.

"You want to come over and talk?"

I stood up and paced the room, measuring one foot carefully in front of the other like an acrobat on a highwire. "I can't. I'm afraid to leave RJ alone. Roger, Hannah as good as admitted to me the other day that RJ has been experimenting with drugs. I was going to take him into the doctor's and get him checked out, but all this other stuff started first."

"So what made you think of it tonight?" he asked. "He looked fine to me this afternoon."

"Well he's stoned now. His eyes are glassy, and he was asleep on the couch when I got here."

"How the hell did he have the time? When did you get there?"

"About a half hour ago. When did you drop them off?"

"Oh," Roger grunted. "He asked to go home early so he wouldn't be interrupted in the middle of the football game."

"So you left them--when? About five?"

"I wasn't looking at my watch, Kaye. But yes, somewhere around then."

"And Hannah was with him?"

"Last I saw. What makes you think he's not just tired?"

I moved in front of the cold bedroom window and looked out without seeing, my nose pressed against the glass. "Roger, come over here and see for yourself. He's out of it. Not only that, but I went into his room and he's got the window wide open to blow the smell out. And there's some kind of pipe full of ashes on the ground outside."

"So now what?"

"I don't know--should I call the police and turn him in?"

"Sure, hand him over to them, why don't you?"

"I want to get him help."

Roger sighed. "Look, it doesn't sound to me like you even have any proof anything is going on."

Enough arguing. I spoke softly but my teeth were definitely clenched. "Roger, I live with this kid. And you see him--what? Twice a week? I'm telling you I think we need to get him looked at--maybe put him into some drug program. Don't you know somebody over at Cenikor?"

"You want to do this tonight?"

"Roger, come see him. Tell me what you think."

"Wait, Kaye. It's obvious that you've had some time to think about all this, but remember I haven't. You come to me with this story about RJ doing drugs, and his blood matching the blood on the backpack and Hannah being mad. That's the only thing I've understood yet, and only because I happened to call last night. When did you think you were going to let me in on all this? Or are you? You still haven't explained about the blood."

"Zack's mother--the boy RJ was with when Elissa died."

"Un huh." He sounded as though he was barely restraining his impatience.

I needed to make this short. I took my nose from the window and started to draw circles on the breath-fogged glass. "She came over here tonight. Zack got hauled in for questioning again, and Detective Deaton told her that they'd typed RJ's blood and it was the same type blood as on the backpack."

"So what? I have the same type blood as RJ. You have the same type blood as RJ. He's type O for God's sake--it's the most prevalent blood type, isn't it? Probably Elissa had type O blood. It doesn't mean anything."

I sagged and reached behind me for the edge of the cot, staggering back to it.

"Kaye?"

I sniffed. "Yes, I'm sorry. I'm here. I... I'd been thinking that myself, but I wasn't sure I was being realistic. This is all such a nightmare."

Roger grunted again. "Well, I'll call Art and let him know. But it sounds to me like the good detective is still fishing, and he's just using different bait. Did you tell Zack's mother that RJ took the blood test because he wanted to help the police find out what happened to Elissa?"

"No, I.... No. I should have. I was still shook up over the drug thing when I heard."

"Okay! Anything else you need to tell me?"

I thought again about seeing Hannah's boyfriend meeting Flynn in the school yard. But what did I really know? "No. That's about it. You coming?"

"I'm coming. Give me some time to call Art about this backpack thing first, before I forget, and I'll try to talk to someone I trust about RJ."

RJ was back on the couch, staring blankly at the TV set when I came out of my room. I stood in the doorway for a moment looking at him, but he didn't react. I went out to the kitchen and drew pictures on that window, waiting until I heard the bell.

Roger's eyes had a couple of lines I hadn't noticed before, but he looked pretty much as he always did. Next to him stood a man I vaguely recognized. He was the director of a drug and alcohol abuse program that Roger had done some accounting work for.

"Can you shut the door? It's cold in here." RJ's voice sounded sulky.

I opened the door wider to let the two men in. "Look RJ, your dad's here," I said brightly.

RJ's dark brows met in the middle of his forehead. He stared deliberately at the television, his jaw set. "I told you I wanted to see this game," he growled.

Roger looked at his friend, who nodded. "RJ," Roger said soothingly. "Do you know Ken Wallenberger? He's a friend of mine. We wanted to talk to you a minute."

We all looked hopefully at RJ, but he ignored us. Ken shook his head, mouth pursed in a firm line. Then he walked over and stood directly in front of RJ blocking his view of the TV set. Ken obviously felt the situation needed a firmer hand than we two pussyfooting parents had. "RJ." His New York accent made the two syllables sound even shorter. "We want you to take a walk with us."

RJ's face grew dark with anger. "All I want is to watch the freakin' football game. This is so screwed up."

Ken nodded. "Yep. The whole world is screwed up. Come on. Take a walk with us. Tell me about it."

I don't know how long they walked. Long enough for me to put in an SOS to Pete anyway. It felt like it took me forever to explain it all. But it didn't take very long before he pulled up into the driveway, snow swirling in his headlights. I flicked on the outside light, then stepped outside onto the stoop in my stocking feet. A flurry of movement further down the walk pulled my eyes.

Under the streetlight, RJ ran, leaving long footprints in the glittering newly laid snow. As he ran, he screamed epithets over his shoulder. Roger trailed far behind. Ken, apparently in better shape, or possibly slightly more prepared for this possibility, sprinted only a few paces behind RJ.

"God, RJ, no!" I ran toward them.

"Mom, stop them." He stopped and screamed the words, looking at me pleadingly. "Dad's freakin' nuts. You know what he wants? He's trying to put me in some freakin' drug program."

Roger stood still a good distance down the street. But Ken reached out a huge hand and spun RJ around before wrestling him down. RJ was still screaming. "Call the cops. This is child abuse. I have rights."

Ken paid little attention that I could see as I drew slowly closer. He pulled RJ's arms behind him, and jerked him upright. "In the state of Colorado, parents have the right to admit their children to a hospital for treatment of drug problems until the child reaches the age of fifteen. You fifteen?"

RJ looked at me then looked down and shook his head.

This was all happening too fast. I chewed hard on my lip, looking at my son's down-turned head. "He's fourteen," I said.

"All right then," Ken said.

Pete got out of his car to stand beside me. "I'm here if you need me," he called to Ken.

Ken shook his head. He pulled RJ upright and looked him straight in the eye. "Behave."

RJ glared back at Ken, then looked at me pleadingly but he stopped struggling. Ken nodded and pushed RJ in the backseat of an unfamiliar black Subaru, buckled him in and flicked a switch on the door before he slammed it closed. Then he looked up at me. "Child protection locks." Without another word, he nodded and got in the driver side of the car.

RJ yelled "Mom!" over the start of Ken's motor.

I wanted to run to him, and pull him out of the car. I wanted to protect him. Was this really the right thing to do? Where were they going? I didn't mean for anything to happen this soon. But if RJ was on drugs... God, what did I mean if? RJ was on drugs.

Pete pulled me into his shoulder and we watched the car drive away. I turned to see where Roger was. Still trudging up the street, as though he was thoroughly tired, or grown old in the walk, he waved the car off with a flick of his hand. It crossed my mind that I hadn't picked the best time to introduce my ex to my what? Boyfriend? Significant other? What do you call the man you're involved with when you're both middle aged? He wasn't my lover. I stifled a small giggle--not sure I wasn't hysterical.

"Roger? This is Pete Farrell. Pete--Roger."

Roger nodded. "The kids told me about you. A policeman, aren't you?"

"That's right," Pete said.

Roger turned his eyes on me, "Not a bad man to know, considering."

What was he implying? That I dated Pete solely to get RJ out of trouble? What did that say about Pete? Or me? I narrowed my eyes. "I don't..."

Pete spoke as affably as though Roger hadn't said a word, "So what now?"

Roger looked at me. "Kaye and I have a couple of things we need to discuss."

"Don't let me hold you up," Pete said.

"Roger, I told him everything," I said.

Roger scowled. "Probably before you bothered discussing it with me."

"Look..."

Pete held up a hand. "If you two want to squabble, let me know, and I'll leave you alone. I thought this was about RJ."

What did Pete mean? Of course this was about RJ. Anything else but the kids was long dead between Roger and me--at least as far as I was concerned.

Pete surveyed us both in silence. "Fine. Now, what's going on?"

"Ken's going to take him in for the night. Do a drug test-- keep him under observation. RJ swears up and down he's not doing anything." Roger threw his head back, and looked up at the sky lit up with snow.

"But?" Pete prodded.

"But..." Roger put his hands to his neck to massage it. "He reeks of some sweet smoky stuff. He's glassy eyed." Roger nodded at me as though to tell me he now understood my assessment. "And Kaye found a pipe and some ashes in back of RJ's open window."

"So maybe marijuana?" I asked. At least that wasn't addictive.

Roger shrugged. "Maybe."

"So after they assess, then what?" I asked.

Roger's jaw was a sharp line, his mouth down turned enough to emphasize the dimple in his chin. "If they find something, then we decide whether we want him to have an inpatient or outpatient program."

This was my area of expertise. I grasped at it. "Inpatient," I said. "Inpatient is better--it gets them out of their regular setting, shakes them up enough to make a difference."

Roger turned away, shoulders still tightly hunched. His voice sounded just as tight when he replied. "It depends on insurance, Kaye. You know that."

I nodded, even though I knew he couldn't see me. So much in the mental health care field depended on money.

* * *

Pete stood next to me on the front stoop. We watched silently as Roger drove off in his car. By then, my feet were painful blocks of ice. All I wanted

111

to do was go inside and hibernate out the winter--alone. One kid in a drug rehab program, the other hiding out from me. God, all I'd ever wanted was to be a good mother. How could I have screwed up so much? I turned and fumbled with the front door, shivering when the warm air hit my cold skin. Pete followed.

I stood awkwardly by the door trying to figure out what to say to him, so I could be alone with my misery. He reached out to take me in his arms, but I shrugged away.

"Now what?" he asked. "Is this where you push me away again, Kaye?"

I hunched a shoulder and flopped down on the couch. Then I made a big show of curling up into the afghan slung over the back. I didn't want to look at him. "I need some time alone."

He followed me to the couch and took my chin in his hand, forcing me to look into his eyes. I felt a rush of irritation, and struggled to get my hand out of my cocoon of blankets and push his hand away, glaring at him.

He said softly, "You were the one who called me here. You must have wanted me then."

My irritation died as quickly as it had risen. I had called him. "I'm sorry." I ran a hand through my hair, and sat up. "I appreciate your coming. I just need some time alone to think."

He nodded, blue eyes fixed solemnly on mine then left without another word. The door clicked loudly as it closed behind him. The house was so quiet. So miserably quiet. I felt numb. Too numb even to cry. Too wired to sleep. I needed to do something. I picked up the phone, not realizing who I was calling until I heard my mother's sleepy voice. "Hello?"

"God, Mom, I'm sorry. It's pretty late there, isn't it?" I glanced at my watch. Surprisingly enough it was still only 8:30 here, though I would have sworn it was midnight. But New Jersey was two hours ahead, and my mother was almost eighty.

"It's all right. I was lying in bed reading," she said. "What's going on?"

I spilled it all, Elissa's murder, RJ's drugs, even Pete. I knew she wouldn't be shocked, and I had to talk. There was nothing my mother hadn't heard-- or maybe done before. Still I felt a bit unnerved when the line fell silent when I got done.

"You did the right thing, Katherine," my mother finally said. "RJ needs help."

Only then did I realize I'd been holding my breath. I expelled it slowly. Yes, that was what worried me the most. "What is the right thing?"

I heard my mother sigh over the phone. "That's the big question when you're raising kids, isn't it?"

I felt a tingle of alarm run through me. Even though her hair was a white cloud and she didn't move as fast as she used to, my mother was strong. Determined. She always felt sure that she knew what was right. Black and white thinking might have been invented by her. Had I done the right thing? Or was she trying to be nice to me--not wanting to hurt my feelings?

"Elissa--the girl who died--went to drug rehab, and it didn't work."

"So you're going to do nothing because it didn't work for one girl? Kaye, you're a therapist. You know better."

"Mom, you should have seen his face. He was calling for me to help him. He's going to feel like I'm rejecting him--like I don't want him."

"It's the drugs you're rejecting, not him." Her sigh came through the line. "I know that you know that though. It's just hard. I worried about the same things, when I went through this with your sister."

She did. Something inside me calmed a bit. Not a lot--but a small easing sensation. My sister had been a hippie way back when hippies were in, and my mother's generation didn't know much about drugs. She must have learned fast. "You did it anyway."

"Put her in the drug program? Certainly I did. Of course she was older and had a choice about it. Not that I told her that. I simply said she was going. And then I took her. And took care of the baby for her while she was in there. There was nothing else I could do, except pray."

God knew I'd never been much at praying. I hung up the phone a few minutes later. Nothing else to do. The words were a litany, echoing through my head. I had to get out of the house. Had to do something. Abruptly I knew what it was. I wanted Hannah to come home. Now. I needed something to be all right with one of my kids.

Chapter 13

I walked out of the house without even my coat. It was a wonder I remembered my purse. The snow had ended, and stars peeked through the scattering clouds. I turned off I-70 at Ward, stopping as the light turned yellow, much to the annoyance of the white Subaru behind me. The driver barely stopped without rear-ending me, and he let me know it, blowing his horn furiously. I just didn't care right then. Let him blow his horn. I had worse problems.

The light wasn't a long one. As I turned North on Ward, the white Subaru turned wide to get around me cutting off a red Chevy in the other lane. The red Chevy's horn blared, but the Subaru just sped up. I saw the guy in the Chevy shrug his shoulders as I zipped past the little auto dealership with the pink concrete pig out front.

Dina opened the door, her plump figure shrouded in a pink chenille bathrobe, huge fuzzy dog slippers on her feet. From the look on her face, the last person she'd expected was me. But then she smiled. "Hey!" she said.

"Hi. I came to get Hannah." The words sounded stiff, and I realized I felt oddly formal with Dina.

"Okay." She said the word slowly as if she felt unsure. Then making up her mind, she said, "Come on in." She pulled the door open wider, the light from behind her spilling out in a broad arc.

Most of the light came from some spotlight thing over by the couch. To me, Dina's furniture looked like something out of Pee Wee's playhouse--on a black and white tv. Everything was gray, oversized--and kind of lumpy in the wrong places. There was probably some fancy designer name for the things--something trendy. I just happened to be the more traditional type. For me, her jungle of plants was the best part of the room.

Hannah lay sprawled on the floor in front of the TV. Her hair spilled over onto the carpet, her plaid pj's the only bright spot in the grey room. I shook my head as I caught sight of what she was watching. The program was some nature thing--probably PBS. That must have been the shock of her life. That was one area where Dina was probably stricter than I'd ever dreamed of being. My kids hadn't seen PBS since they'd grown too old for Sesame street. I grinned.

Hannah caught me at it, looking up at just that moment and scowling darkly. "Hello, Mother." She turned pointedly back to the program.

I stood awkwardly for a moment, trying to decide what to do. Dina hovered nervously in the doorway, obviously unsure about whether to leave us alone to talk or to help me out. Screw it! I stood in front of the TV and flicked it off.

Hannah sat up abruptly. "What are you doing?" she asked coldly.

I sat down in one of the oddly shaped gray chairs, my eyes on hers. "I want you to come home. So we need to talk."

Dina nodded and smiled, her decision made for her. She headed down the hall toward the bedrooms.

"About what?" Hannah pivoted on her butt, toward me, bending her knees and leaning her chin on them. "You were a total jerk, Mother."

"Because I don't want boys in the house when I'm not there? I don't think so."

"This isn't about boys. There aren't any boys. Only Josh. What do you think we're doing? Having orgies? You have no trust in me."

"I have plenty of trust in you. It's Josh I don't trust."

Hannah's nostrils flared, a sure sign that she was ticked and trying to get a rein on it. She didn't succeed. "That's retarded," she sputtered. "What do you think is going on?"

I strove for calm. "I don't know what's going on. I'm not there. For all I know, he's selling drugs to your brother." I hadn't intended to get into this, but suddenly I didn't care.

"Josh!" She burst out laughing. "That is so stupid. He can't stand drugs. That's why he's always having a problem with... and what makes you think RJ is buying drugs?"

I raised my eyebrows. "Come on, Hannah. We talked about this the other day."

She widened her eyes. "I think you must be thinking of someone else, Mother."

I leaned forward in the chair, almost in her face. "The other day, in the field, when we saw Flynn. I asked you if RJ was involved with drugs, and you gasped."

She shrugged. "So?"

"So, now you're trying to say he doesn't do drugs?" My voice rose on the last part of the sentence.

Hannah glanced uneasily around as though afraid Dina had heard. I didn't give a damn. As a matter of fact, it might be a relief to talk to Dina about all this. She had a level head, and probably knew a lot more about drugs than I did.

"I'm not saying anything," Hannah finally said. She set her mouth in a straight firm line and deliberately looked away from me.

"Oh, great, Hannah. Anything so you can feel like you didn't tattle, is that it? Is that the best thing for your brother and Josh? And what about Flynn? He's in this waist deep, and you'd better believe I'm going to be talking to his mother."

She stood up abruptly, leaning over to shout into my face. "Yeah, so what? Everyone knows Flynn's into drugs. I never said he wasn't. You want to tell his mother--go ahead. She'd have to be wasted herself not to know anyway. But why do you have to keep dragging Josh into this? Josh didn't do anything except stay over at our house a couple of times when you weren't there."

"I saw Josh behind Lawrence Elementary School, tonight. With Flynn." I spaced the words out clearly and evenly.

Hannah straightened up, brow knit. "So?"

"I saw something change hands there, Hannah. Now think. They weren't in the playground of an empty elementary school to trade baseball cards."

Hannah shook her head. "You don't understand. It wasn't what you think. Flynn's a dealer, yeah. And if you must know, I did think RJ was doing some--some experimenting. But Josh..." She shook her head.

"Experimenting? Is that what you call it?"

She shrugged and sat down on the floor again, not looking at me.

I could tell by looking at her she knew it was more than that. My heart sank. Until then, I had hoped... "Why didn't you tell me?" I whispered. My eyes were stinging and wet.

She hunched a shoulder, but didn't look up. Instead she traced a pattern in the carpet with her fingers. Over and over, just a circle.

I reached out a finger to her chin, trying without success to tilt her head up. "Come home, Hannah. I need you and I think you need me."

She jerked her head away from me. Then looked up to let me see the anger sparking her blue eyes. "This is the way you wanted it, Mom. If you'd only trusted me, I wouldn't be here." Then her own eyes teared up. She jumped up and ran out of the room.

Where did she get off doing that? She couldn't just walk off like that. I clenched my teeth together and started down the hall after her. Dina appeared in the hallway, short blond hair standing up to reveal her dark roots. She tightened the belt on her robe. "Let her go, Kaye," she said.

I blew air out of my mouth hard, and darted around Dina. "I can't." I tossed the words over my shoulder.

She grabbed me by the elbow in what seemed an automatic gesture. Her grip was firm on my arm. My panting was the only break in the silence. Finally, I met Dina's dark eyes.

"Let her go, Kaye," she said softly.

"She's lied to me, deceived me, and flat out flouted my rules, and now I'm just supposed to let it all go?"

"Lied to you about what?"

"RJ, Josh, you name it."

Dina slanted an eyebrow at me. "Kaye, I couldn't help but hear..."

I nodded. "You and the rest of the neighborhood."

Dina grinned. "It wasn't that bad really. But nothing I heard made me think Hannah lied to you."

I tilted my head, studying Dina. Perspective on parenting from someone I respected was rare. Like most, I operated on gut and instinct, but rarely did I get any feedback. My gut told me something was off in that conversation with Hannah. She still wasn't telling me something. But here was Dina, the objective outsider, saying something different. I would listen. But gut and instinct were strong.

"What about Josh?" I asked.

Dina waved me back toward the lighted living room. I walked slowly, looking back at her the whole way. She sat in one of the gray chairs, hooking her feet into her robe and tucking them under her. I flopped in the opposite chair, keeping my eyes intently on her.

"What about Josh?" she asked.

"She was deceitful all the way along about Josh. She had him there nights when I told her not to. She's probably sleeping with him. And don't tell me that she doesn't know what drugs he's into."

Dina frowned, making her round face all down turned lines. "I got the impression she didn't think Josh did any drugs. It sounded like she was telling the truth about that to me, Kaye. At least the truth as she knows it."

I snorted, and sat back in the chair, crossing my legs.

Dina eyed me thoughtfully. "This isn't really what you're upset about anyway. Josh is just a side issue now. You wanted her to tell you about RJ."

Tears stung my eyes and I turned to study the ceiling, hoping to blink them away. "Is that such an odd idea?"

Dina grabbed a box off the table next to me and handed me a tissue, without ever taking her eyes from me. "She did find a way to let you know, even though it got her into more trouble."

Yeah right. Hannah let me know only when I pried it out of her. This conversation was leading nowhere. No way was I going to let someone, even a good friend, tell me I didn't know what I knew. I rubbed the tissue irritably at my eyes and nose, then stood up and headed for the door. "It's not done yet, Dina. I'll let her go tonight. But I know there's something she's not telling me. You tell her I'll be back." I didn't wait for Dina's response--just let the door close softly behind me.

Since the snow had stopped, the temperature had dropped big time. The windows of my car were frosted. Naturally, I couldn't find the scraper. I debated asking Dina for one, but I didn't want to go back in that house.

I dug deep into my wallet and pulled out my Visa card, scraping awkwardly at the windshield with the side of the card. It worked. My gloveless hands hurt with the cold and I started to shiver violently, since I'd forgotten my coat. But I took some pride in getting that windshield clear enough to look out of. The cold didn't cool my thoughts though. My brain raced. I knew what I had to do.

It looked to me as though we had a thread here. RJ, Flynn and, no matter what Hannah said, Josh, were somehow involved in drugs. And Thea had complained that Elissa was on drugs the day she disappeared. There had to be a connection. I hadn't gotten it out of Hannah, but I wouldn't let that stop me. I was going to see Thea.

It wasn't far, distance wise. Thea lived in my old neighborhood--maybe three miles from Dina. But it was a whole different world. The houses got bigger the closer I got. That was okay. Bigger can be better.

But the houses in that neighborhood were huge pseudo-Victorian monstrosities with garages that rivaled the living space. The yards, dwarfed by the structures, glittered with Christmas lights. I'd moved out of this subdivision less than a year ago. I should have felt as though I was coming home. Instead I felt alienated. Why had I never noticed how alike all these houses were? If it weren't for paint colors and yard ornaments, they'd be impossible to tell apart.

I pulled up in the short drive next to my old house. Only after I rang the bell did I think to look at my watch. 9:30. I shrugged. I'd seen Thea and George up later. The door opened soundlessly. A small forlorn figure peered cautiously out.

My God! Thea? I had to stifle a gasp at the change in her.

Her huge, shadowed, dark eyes almost swallowed her face. The lounging pajamas she wore seemed too big for her tiny frame and her usually shiny dark hair hung lank and uncombed. "Kaye," she said and opened the door wider with a wobbly attempt at a smile.

Way to go, Kaye! I berated myself silently. This poor woman just lost her daughter. Her only child. And you won't even let her rest. "Thea, God, I'm sorry," I babbled. "I just didn't think. I'll call you tomorrow." I started to turn away, ready to dive down the steps and slink into a hole.

Thea pulled gently on my sleeve. "No, Kaye. It's all right. Really. Come in and have a drink."

A drink? I didn't remember ever being offered one at Thea's house before. Her husband, George, was a teetotaler. He told the world he was a reformed drunk.

Thea must have seen my expression. "George is away on business. He's always away on business." She brooded on that a minute, then abruptly brightened. "He'll neither know nor care." She giggled a little then turned down the long mirror-lined hall--leaving me to shut the door and follow. I wanted to leave. I shouldn't have been there in the first place; I knew that when I saw Thea's face. And her odd behavior confirmed it. What should I do? This was not the woman I knew.

Apparently, it hadn't occurred to her that I might not accept her invitation. She'd walked off down the hall without looking back. I followed her as expected into the living room.

This at least was familiar ground. I'd spent a lot of time in this room with George and Thea, and the room hadn't changed in the least. The white damask sofa was as pristine as the last time I'd seen it--probably as pristine as the day it left the furniture store. The cherry end tables gleamed in the light of the polished brass lamps. The wing chairs that flanked the couch were still upholstered in a leafy celedon print.

But over it all hung the smell of alcohol. A puddle marred the sheen of the wood floor by the antique secretary. On its top, a crystal decanter lay overturned. Thea hovered over the mess, dabbing at it ineffectively with a tissue.

"Let me get something for that, Thea," I said, turning back into the hallway toward the kitchen, where I knew I would find paper towels.

"I've got it," Thea called after me, sounding peevish.

It was clear from her voice. She didn't want my help. But that wasn't the reason I stopped dead in my tracks. The kitchen stank of old garbage. Dishes crusted with dried food lined the sink. A milk container left out too long stood open on the counter. Next to it, empty booze bottles crowded the space. The refrigerator was slightly ajar, and I moved to close it. My shoes stuck to the floor. Its usual immaculate surface was tacky with some thick dark stuff spilled on it.

I turned to leave, only to see Thea's stricken face in the door. "I told you. I've got it," she said loudly.

I nodded silently. What could I say? She pushed past me and reached to the spool on the counter for the paper towels, only to find it empty. With a curse, she spun around and reached under the sink where I knew from long experience she kept the extras. Again she came up empty. I reached over the filthy counter top, and grabbed a handful of napkins from their holder and held them out to her. She grabbed them with a muttered thanks that sounded almost like a curse, and flew back out of the room.

I stood astounded. I knew of course, that grief took people different ways, and Thea had had a terrible loss. But I didn't even know this woman. This house, like her person, always looked spotless. And she and George seemed to be so close. That had been the one thing to be thankful for in all this. They had each other. How long had he been gone on this "business trip"? It was obvious that she'd been drinking for a while. I stood in the reeking kitchen, just thinking. Should I try to talk to her? But no, I shook my head. There really was no good way to talk to someone as drunk as she must be. The best thing I could do for her was to leave, and let her sleep this off.

A crashing sound from the direction of the living room interrupted my thoughts. Thea yelled something I couldn't make out. I ran toward the living room, sure she must be hurt. "What happened? Are you okay, Thea?"

She stood over a lamp lying on the floor, the other lamp raised high in her arms. Obviously, she was ready to throw it down to join the other.

"Thea, no." I called out, running to grab the lamp.

She glared at up me from under her tousled hair. "What the hell do I care about some lamp?" she said in a low voice. "What do you care? How could you let this happen, Kaye? How could you let RJ do this to my little girl?" Her face twisted. She let the lamp slip from her grasp and collapsed on the floor beside it, sobbing.

"Thea, please. RJ didn't do this. You know he didn't-- couldn't have ever--hurt Elissa. He adored her." I slipped into the room, my hand out, begging her to believe me. All the time, I was praying that what I was saying was true. RJ couldn't have hurt Elissa, could he?

Thea's eyes glittered. "Right, Kaye. Real damn great way he's got of showing that. I know they're thinking of arresting that friend of his. Cop came to the door to tell me. That Zeke didn't do it alone, Kaye. Now, did he? Answer me that."

My God! She hated me. Hated RJ. She really believed he did it. But she wasn't making any sense. Was she like this when the cop came? "They didn't arrest Zack," I said emphasizing his name.

"Zeck, Zack, Zeb. What does it matter? They'll get him."

Maybe this was my opening. I wanted to tell her about Flynn and my suspicions about him, the drugs that both Elissa and RJ seemed to be involved with--everything. "Thea, I don't think either of the boys did it. I need your help to prove that. I think..."

Thea waved a hand and barked out a throaty laugh. "You think. Just what do you think? You don't know. You don't know anything. You probably don't even know yet that RJ is up to his neck in this drug crap. Just like Elissa."

She knew? Did everyone know before me? My eyes stung. "Yes, yes, I do." I whispered.

She nodded, looking at me with narrowed eyes. "Yeah, you do now, don't you? When did you find out, I wonder? Did the kid have to smoke his pipe right in front of your nose?" She shook her head laughing and rocking herself. Only when she started to sniff did I realize she was still crying, too. Then she stopped and looked up at me, dark eyes flashing again with that incredible anger.

"Thea, please. Let me call someone to be with you."

She laughed, stepping quietly closer the whole time. "Concerned, are you? Where was your concern before? Why didn't you keep that druggie son of yours locked up?" She picked up a letter opener from the table, holding it above her head. "If the cops came now, and found you," she dropped her voice to an almost friendly conversational level. "I could say it was self-defense. I'd tell them you threatened me. And they'd believe me, because, after all, who's the victim here?" She took a long, lunging step coming abruptly, disconcertingly closer, the letter opener still held in position to strike. "You came here to try to get me to feel sorry for your lousy murdering son? I don't."

I shook my head again and backed up hastily and bumped into the doorframe. Then I scooted around it and ran. I didn't stop until I reached the car.

I heard her behind me, laughing in the cold still night air. She called to me from the front doorstep. "Don't come back, Kaye. You never know what will happen then."

Chapter 14

I drove around in the car after that. For hours. I didn't want to go home to my empty house. Didn't want to go see Pete. Didn't want to wake my mother up again. I didn't feel like sleeping. I'd left Hannah with my best friend. What was there to do, but drive around?

It wasn't that I had a lot of energy either. I just felt numb. Was this what a state of shock felt like? I'd seen it enough with the safe house residents; I should be able to identify it in myself. Okay, so maybe I was in a state of shock. Who wouldn't be in my circumstances? My son, a suspect in a murder case, had been taken to a drug rehab center, and my daughter had run away to a friend's house and wouldn't come home. And my friend, Thea, had been driven to the point of complete mental and physical devastation. Due to what? My son? Oh, God, my son.

I don't know how long I drove. I paid no attention. Finally I found myself going through a long tunnel. I hate tunnels--especially at night. The bright lights of the other side helped me identify the Eisenhower tunnel. I couldn't remember how I got there. I turned around when I got to the after-hours calm of the factory outlet in Silverthorne. There was no place to turn before that.

I drove right back to where I started--or at least next door. Without even thinking about it, I drove to my old house-- right next to Thea's. With a wary eye on the neighbor, I rang the bell on the door to Roger's house.

Roger looked fresh out of the shower, his dress shirt crisp, and unbuttoned at the collar, his black suit pants had a razor like crease. "Kaye? You look awful. Come in."

I shook my head. Suddenly I wasn't sure what to say or really why I had come. He knew as much as I did about the kids. And what could he do about Thea? "Thea thinks RJ killed Elissa."

Roger's face darkened, his mouth in a grim line. "Thea can't get her nose out of a bottle long enough to know what she thinks."

"You knew?"

Roger snorted. "It's obvious to anyone who sees her."

"Does George know?"

Roger shrugged. "I couldn't tell you. I haven't seen George."

Oh, God. So things were bad there, too. "Roger, we need to get her help. No wonder she's like this--with Elissa dead and all."

Roger shook his head, his mouth a grim line. "Kaye, you always want to save the world. Did it ever occur to you that some people aren't worth saving? Thea had problems before Elissa died. Let's worry about our own problems first, okay?"

* * *

I still didn't want to be home even when I turned into the driveway. The house lights blazed into the dark night. I stood on the front step with the door open in front of me, for the longest time, just trying to make myself walk into the living room. Roger was right. I needed to concentrate on my own problems first. But I couldn't face them. The house was so empty.

Finally I shut the door and turned out the lights. Then I threw myself on that miserable uncomfortable cot in my room, and cried until my head ached so badly, I felt nauseated. I couldn't sleep. I lay there for long hours shivering until I could tell myself I had to get up. But I had nothing to get up for. It was Sunday. My day off with the kids. What a laugh.

I had to do something. I had to find something to do. I couldn't believe everything that had happened last night. What had I thought I was doing? First, I put RJ in drug rehab, then I confronted Hannah, then Thea. And I'd thought Thea was crazy. Well she was. I'd been physically afraid of her, something I never remembered ever being before. Could grief really do that?

Even if she was totally insane, in her misery she'd known more than I did about RJ and the drugs. But she had to be wrong about him hurting Elissa. She was wrong. RJ would never hurt Elissa. I knew that last night, and I'd tried to tell Thea.

I'd thought about it all night. RJ had taken the blood test. He'd told me he didn't do it. I was his mother. I had to believe him. I had to support him.

I called the drug rehab center as soon as it was decently light. It must have been all of 7:30.

"Bright Harvest."

It sounded like an organic food store or a cafeteria. I choked on the thought, suddenly unprepared for my turn to talk. "Uh, my son was taken there last night by Ken Wallenberger. I was wondering if I could talk to him." Great, that sounded really clear. She probably thought I wanted to talk to Ken.

"I'm sorry." Her voice actually sounded sorry. It wasn't the professional sorry I've developed when I have to give people news they didn't want to hear. She sounded truly concerned. "We have a policy of no contact for 72 hours when a boy is admitted here."

"Seventy-two hours? We don't even know if he's on drugs yet."

"We only admitted one boy last night, so I'm guessing RJ is your son."

I grunted my agreement.

"I have to tell you the report seems to indicate he showed many of the signs. He was extremely combative and confrontational. His eyes were red and unfocused, and his coordination was off."

Why was this so hard to hear? I'd known this.

Her voice was soft and gentle. "I think it seems pretty clear. You must think so, too, or he wouldn't be here."

I wanted to cry. Of course, I'd known it. But here was a professional assessment. "Seventy-two hours," I said again softly, more to try to get myself used to the idea than anything else.

"Yes. We believe that it's better for both the teen and the parent to come to terms with the teen's problem separately. At the end of that time, we do an assessment, together with the drug test results, and recommend a course of treatment."

This I recognized as her professional spiel. She had it down so she could say it in her sleep, all in that soothing tone guaranteed to calm a terrified parent. "Do parents participate in the assessments?"

"Absolutely. We welcome parental input. As a matter of fact, we require it. It takes a whole family working together to beat a drug problem. You will be contacted by your son's caseworker. He or she will set up the appointment with you."

"That would be Tuesday night or Wednesday then," I said woodenly.

"Yes. Are there any other questions I can answer for you?"

"No. I...thank you." I set the phone down and sank into one of the kitchen chairs. Tuesday or Wednesday. I'd go out of my mind before then.

What could I do? I needed to do something. Dully, I gulped a couple of aspirin and headed for the shower. Maybe I could think better if I cleaned up and got rid of my headache.

The steamy water worked like a medicine, opening up the sinuses my long night of crying had clogged up. I soaped off slowly.

If I questioned Flynn about the drugs, would he tell me anything? He seemed to be right smack in the middle of this. But no, I shook my head slowly; I'd have to take him by surprise somehow. I didn't know even what drugs we were talking about yet and, with Flynn, knowledge was definitely power. When the time came, I might have to confront Anita about Flynn's drug use first and then together we could tackle him.

So there was only one person left who I could talk to about this. And I even knew where I might be able to snare him and his mother in one smooth catch. I was going to church. Maybe not the Catholic church my mother wanted me in, but church.

Josh went to the 10:30 youth service over at Arvada Christian Church. He and Hannah had gone together more than once. Wouldn't my mother be proud? I could pray and pry at the same time.

I was on the still snowy doorstep slamming the locked door when a truck pulled up in front of the house, shining in the chilly sun. Pete got out and strolled toward me, his sunglasses hiding his eyes from me.

I abruptly felt fragile again, all my purpose oozing out of me. I didn't think I could stand it if he wanted to talk about last night or even commented that he'd never heard of me going to church as long as he'd known me. I turned to face him with my jaw set, knowing my red-rimmed eyes would tell their own story. "I'm going to service," I said by way of greeting.

He nodded affably. "Want some company?"

And suddenly, I did. "It's the youth service over at Arvada Christian," I said, as if that would make him change his mind.

"You driving, or am I?"

I sat in his truck, and tucked my coat around me carefully. I hadn't been to any church in quite a while. A fundamentalist one, never. I could only hope my wool slacks and sweater would be considered dressy enough. "So did you come just to take me to church?" I asked, looking at Pete.

He shrugged lightly. "If that's what you want."

I couldn't stand it. I wanted to talk about us and last night and RJ and drugs, but I didn't. I absolutely hated the idea that Pete didn't have to talk about it.

"I believe him, you know." I turned my face straight ahead to the slushy road, for all the world as though I were the one driving.

"Believe who?" He fiddled with the defrost for a moment directing the heat away from the windshield and onto us.

My frozen feet thanked him. "I believe RJ. I don't think he killed Elissa."

"That so?" Pete straightened up and put both his hands on the wheel. He had his cop mask on.

I watched him carefully without turning toward him. Six months ago I wouldn't have been able to read his face. Now I knew from the way he said that, and his sudden careful attention to driving that he didn't agree with me. My heart sank, but I concentrated on outlining my reasons to him, hoping to sway him with what I hoped was my logic. "You don't know him. But he's really a pretty good kid. He'd never hurt anybody--certainly not Elissa. He got the blood test because he wanted to prove it. He didn't kill her."

"And what do you think about the drugs?" Pete turned to look at me quickly and then flicked his gaze back to the road.

I shook my head, tears stinging my eyes. I brushed awkwardly at them with the back of hand and sniffed. "I'm not stupid, Pete. I know he's doing something. But he told me he would never hurt Elissa, and I believe him." I turned my knees toward Pete, facing him as well as I could face him considering he was driving. "I'm not taking him out of the rehab center. He's where he belongs. But he didn't kill Elissa. Just because he's doing drugs doesn't mean he's a murderer."

He nodded. "And we're going to church because... you want to pray about it?"

I smiled, sniffed again and shook my head. "It probably wouldn't hurt... but I'm going to church to find Hannah's boyfriend, Josh. I want to talk to him. "

"About Hannah?"

"About Hannah, and RJ and drugs and Flynn."

"Flynn." Pete shook his head.

"Flynn is a kid whose mother is staying at Beginnings. He's been there with her before and frankly none of the counselors can stand him." I paused a minute trying to pick my words carefully and finally decided just to plunge in. "He's into drugs--maybe a dealer. And both my kids know him and that scares the stuffing out of me. Turns out he was Elissa's boyfriend. And Josh knows him, too. I saw him with Flynn last night outside of Lawrence Elementary school."

"So you're going to talk to Josh about last night or about drugs or what? About Elissa?" Pete sounded genuinely perplexed.

I felt relieved. That had to be a sign that he couldn't stay professionally detached. I shook my head. "I don't know. Maybe. It just seems like this whole drug thing is a thread that runs through this. Josh is involved somehow. Maybe he knows something."

"And if he doesn't want to talk?"

I chewed on my bottom lip, and said slowly, "I'm hoping his parents will be at church. Maybe we can put our heads together."

Pete laughed shortly. "Way to go, Kaye. I wouldn't mess with you if I were him." He turned and flicked a speculative look at me. "And if RJ did it, under the influence of drugs?" he asked softly.

I winced. "Then I need to know that. But I don't think he did."

Arvada Christian was a beige brick church with a huge steeple and beautiful stained-glass windows. I'd driven past it many times. Today the parking lot was so full that cars lined the streets blocks away.

After our hike in the cold, the sanctuary's warmth felt good. The sounds of an organ and a choir came from the closed double doors directly across from the entrance. But the usher directed us to the stairs. Youth service was downstairs.

The bare wooden steps led to a huge tiled room filled with folding chairs facing a stage. We were early, only the kids in the band, and the kids who did the greeting were there when we arrived. That was what Hannah liked about this service. The youth group did everything but the sermon. The youth pastor did that.

I chose seats toward the back so I could watch who came in. Slinging my legs crossways on the chair, I kept my back toward Pete so that I had a view of the door, and most of the basement.

The room slowly filled with chattering teens, some with their families, many with friends. All the kids appeared to know one another. I was surprised to recognize the two shaven-headed girls from Elissa's memorial service, still wearing long black skirts. They didn't seem like religious types somehow. But I guessed that was my own perception of religion coming out.

The guitarist struck a chord, and the blonde boy at the keyboard with the skater haircut nodded, tapped his foot in time and swung into the opening hymn. It wasn't one I recognized, but the words were soothing. Something about giving all your cares to Jesus. Jesus could have my cares. He was welcome to them. The problem was I wasn't sure He would take care of my son the way I wanted Him to. I sighed and stirred restlessly.

My mother would be sure those feelings were heresy. Luckily, she couldn't know how I really felt about God. She'd be horrified to know how angry I was with Him. I blinked back the stinging liquid in my eyes. The word anger didn't cover the half of it really. I felt God screwed up. If I were God, things would be different.

My mother would be appalled that I even had those thoughts.

Absorbed in my own funk, I'd about given up on Josh and his parents when I saw his long, lanky form, encased in the usual jeans and purple high school letter jacket, ambling toward me. No parents. I felt a pang of disappointment.

At about the same time, I noticed a tiny brunette giggling with a couple of other girls just two rows behind me. She wore a spaghetti strap dress more suitable for summer than a snowy November. I don't know how I missed her before. She was such a cute little thing. Her whole face lit up when she saw Josh. She got up from her seat and started toward him. He shook his head at her and waved, ambling just past me to a seat on the aisle.

I watched the brunette stick her lip out in disappointment before I swiveled around on my seat. I wanted to lean forward and buttonhole Josh right then. If nothing else, I wanted to ask if Hannah knew the brunette. But the whole congregation stood up and swung into a rousing rendition of "Keep your eyes on Jesus."

Pete pulled me up to stand with them. The service seemed to take forever.

* * *

I didn't let the strains of the ending song die away before I stepped forward to grab Josh. Pete could fend for himself. I figured parents or no, I still wanted to talk to Josh. And if I waited for the end of the song, that brunette would beat me to him. "I want to talk to you," I said, tapping him on the shoulder.

"Oh hi, K... Ms. Berreano."

At least he'd remembered to call me that. I smiled with satisfaction. One lecture I'd made to one kid had gotten through.

"What can I do for you?" he asked.

Right on cue, the little brunette floated up. "Hi, Josh," she cooed. The look on her face was that of someone who beholds God. Somehow, I doubted that it had anything to do with the service.

Josh smiled in a carefully polite way, and spoke in that voice adults use to young and not very intelligent children. "Hi, Tiffany. Nice service."

Tiffany flushed to the depths of her dress's neckline--a long way. Then she giggled.

Josh apparently expected nothing else because he nodded, and said, "See you at school tomorrow, okay?"

Tiffany nodded, and giggled again. Josh turned and strolled up the aisle toward a side door I hadn't noticed before. I decided that in this crowd, I'd better stay glued to his side. So with a quick glance back over the heads of the congregation to make sure Pete saw where I was going, I darted over to follow Josh. Pete waved affably to me through the congregation. I took that to mean he was coming.

The glare of sunlight hurt my eyes after the building's darkness. The parking lot looked no less busy than the basement where the youth service was held. Two tall boys were playing keep-away with the hair tie of a shrieking red-head. Clumps of teens stood talking. A girl from one group tried to catch Josh's attention.

What did all these girls see in this guy? He was just another tall skinny kid.

Josh appeared oblivious. He stopped just a few feet away from the church door, and turned to face me. "Sorry about that," he waved back toward the church, his face red. "I think she has a crush on me."

I nodded gravely, even though that had to be the understatement of the year. "Does Hannah know?" I asked.

Josh nodded, screwing his mouth to one side. "That's why Hannah comes to church with me sometimes. We see Tiffany at school, you know? But Hannah says Tiffany needs to be reminded who my girlfriend is."

That sounded like Hannah all right. Poor Tiffany was lucky Hannah wasn't really angry. "I'm sure Hannah will handle Tiffany," I murmured sweetly.

Pete came up behind me and gave my shoulder a squeeze, making a noise behind me that sounded half way between a cough and a laugh. "Oh, yeah. Hannah will handle her all right. She'll steamroll right over Tiffany," he whispered in my ear.

I narrowed my eyes at him. After all, it was one thing for me to think such things about my daughter and another for him to. I made a mental note to talk to him about that later. I hoped what I really thought wasn't quite as obvious to Josh. But enough time wasting. This wasn't why I came. "Josh, I need to talk to you."

He raised his eyebrows good-naturedly.

I hurriedly shook my head. "Not here." I gestured to the crowded parking lot. "Let's go get some breakfast or something."

Josh smiled. "There's a place in Old Town that does a great latte."

"Wonderful," I drawled, turning and smiling at Pete.

From his expression, I guessed he was about to gag. He was probably the only person on earth who hated all these trendy coffee places more than I did.

I turned back toward Josh and gestured. "Do you know Pete Farrell?"

* * *

I finally figured out why I avoided restaurants after church on Sunday. All those people who go to church end up out for breakfast afterwards. We walked down the street from the church to what looked like a small cottage. It had lace curtains, a wrought iron fence and a line of people out the door. We fought our way through the crowd to give the hostess our names.

The floors were wood, the warmth was inviting and the enticing aroma of coffee hung over all. The bakery case held some really decadent looking cinnamon rolls along with an assortment of pies and cakes. Above it hung what looked like a good breakfast menu. Obviously, this was not the usual marble table coffee shop with biscotti and scones.

I raised my eyebrow at Pete behind Josh's back, and he smiled back at me. This place looked great. Unfortunately it seemed the rest of the Denver metro area had figured that out before us. We sat on a frozen curb outside for twenty minutes with all the other customers waiting for a seat. Obviously not the place for a private chat.

The curb's cold crept under my coat. The sunlight bouncing off the snow made me narrow my eyes against the brightness. So I leaned into Pete's warmth, shivering and squinting, making small talk with Josh. What were his plans for the holidays?

By the time the hostess called us in, I was becoming steadily more convinced that I must have been mistaken about Josh. He chattered away about National honor society meetings and his work with his church youth group. It was obvious, even to me, that something else must have been going on at that elementary school. Boy Scout meetings and escorting little old ladies across the street were the worst things I could accuse him of.

The hostess led us to a sturdy oak table next to one of the lace-curtained windows. The sunlight, magnified by the window, made a little puddle of warmth on the blue checked cushioned seat. The waitress hustled right over with our menus and a coffee pot that she set right on the table after pouring us each a cup. I wrapped my hands around the cup and just inhaled. The smell alone was worth the wait. Pete's eyes met mine over the cup. He smiled and nodded to urge me on.

Okay, time to get on with it. I took a cautious sip of steaming coffee. I needed something to fortify me for the discussion with Josh. My doubts by that time made me shaky.

"Josh?" I said softly, to break the trance he seemed to be in.

His eyes snapped back into focus immediately.

"I had hoped your parents would be at church with you."

He hunched one shoulder, the corner of his mouth drooping just a bit. "My dad moved to Grand Junction a couple of months ago, and my mom's not much of a church goer. I used to go with my grandma, but she died last year."

Boy, had I fallen down on the job. I prided myself on knowing all the parents of my kids' important friends, but I hadn't realized his parents were divorced. I'd met his parents, of course--several times. It had never dawned on me that it had always been one or the other--never both at the same time.

"You must have been close to your Grandma," Pete said.

Josh nodded; his eyes got that far away look again. "She was great, you know, just like in the story books. She baked cookies for me and took me places. I miss her a lot."

I took another sip of coffee and watched him, my doubts mounting. Still, why had he met Flynn at the elementary school? I had to know. I might not be able to alert his parents that there was a problem, but I could at least get some answers.

The waitress materialized to take our order. Not at all prepared, I blurted out the first thing I could think of. "I'll take one of those cinnamon rolls."

Pete's eyes twinkled, as he virtuously ordered a veggie omelet made with egg whites only and a side of fruit. Josh, hesitated, looking at me from the corner of his eyes.

Finally I figured out that he probably didn't have much money. "Eat what you want, Josh," I said. "I'm paying. I asked you to come for breakfast."

Pete's eyebrows rose and he smiled. "I should have ordered more."

I tilted my nose deliberately in the air as though I were offended and gestured toward the waitress. "Hey, she could still change your order. Go for it," I said briskly.

Josh looked back and forth between our faces, before apparently deciding that we were teasing. He smiled. "I'll have the North West skillet."

The waitress smiled back at him and bustled off.

"Hey, and I was going to get steak and eggs," said Pete.

I wrinkled my nose at him. "Next time."

Josh was still shaking his head at us when I decided to plunge in.

"Josh, why did you meet Flynn Connors at the playground last night?"

Josh's skin turned pink and his eyes widened, but he didn't look at me. "What playground?" he asked in a casual tone.

I turned to look at Pete. For the first time that morning, he held his mouth in a straight line.

Softly but firmly I said, "Josh, I saw you with Flynn last night. I know that he's involved with drugs. Are you?"

Josh turned hard eyes to me. "Is that what you think? Is that why you wanted to talk to my parents?"

I decided to answer carefully. No point in saying what I'd really thought. I didn't want to scare him off by telling him I wondered if he were involved with this mess with Elissa. "I have to ask. As to your parents, I want to talk to them about your spending the night at my house with my daughter when I'm not there."

His pink color deepened to crimson. "It's not what you think."

Was he embarrassed or angry? I couldn't tell from his tone. I decided to muddle on. "Josh, you don't know what I think. I want you to answer my question--as it is I'm going to have to go talk to your mother. Are you involved in drugs?"

Josh stood up, his face contorted, and his teeth bared, leaving me in no doubt now about his emotions. I was glad that I wasn't alone with him.

"My mother..." breathing hard, he emphasized the word mother, "already knows that I met with Flynn the other night. If you want to know about it so badly, you'll just have to go ask her."

He turned and almost knocked the bench over getting out. Heads turned in the restaurant as he stomped out the door.

Chapter 15

Pete searched my face, obviously worried about me. "You okay?"

After last night, a kid storming off could hardly faze me--especially if he wasn't my kid. But I'd be glad to eat and get out of there. People were staring. "I'm fine."

"Now what?"

"We eat?"

Pete smiled. "A woman with the proper perspective. And then after we eat?"

I knew what I was going to do. I was going to Josh's house, but I didn't want to tell Pete that and have him argue with me. I shook my head and sighed. "I go home, I guess."

Pete's expression eased. "I still don't get what you were hoping to do here. He seems like a nice kid. You don't usually find drug addicts going to church on Sunday. And how does all this connect with RJ and Elissa? Or are you just getting on Josh's case because he stayed with Hannah a couple of nights when you weren't there?"

"No." I struggled to find the words to tell him what I was trying to do. "Mostly, I'm operating on instinct, I guess. It's not that I think Josh killed Elissa."

I frowned, trying to organize my thoughts well enough for him to follow. In the process, I realized, I hadn't brought him up to date on what happened the night before. "I went to see Hannah last night after you left. I wanted her home. She wouldn't come though. She was pretty angry with me. And I got pretty mad, too. So I told her about Josh meeting Flynn." I took a sip of coffee, and let my gaze wander out the window to the busy antiques section of Olde Town Arvada. "She didn't seem surprised. She wasn't worried about Josh doing anything wrong either." I glanced back toward Pete. "I've always trusted her judgment--she's never given me reason not to. So I want to believe that Josh is okay. But he is involved with Flynn. And somehow Flynn is involved with all of this." I waved a hand.

Pete's eyebrows met in the middle of his forehead. "So you were hoping to scare Josh into telling you something about Flynn?"

Suddenly miserably tired, I let myself slump. "I don't know. Maybe. I know enough about Flynn to know he's not going to tell me anything unless I use a crowbar to pry it out of him. But I know Flynn has some sort of drug connection. Even Hannah admits that. And I know Flynn was Elissa's boyfriend. And both RJ and Josh have some link to Flynn that I don't understand."

"And what will all that get you?"

"I don't know." I stared into Pete's blue eyes, wondering whether to tell him about Thea. It was just sinking in that she'd threatened me--something that would definitely arouse Pete's protective side. But maybe he could figure out how all this fit together. "It's like I know something--or forgot something that will help me figure all this out. I don't know what it is. But right now, I've got to keep looking."

"Right now, what you look is tired." Pete reached out to capture my hands in his. "There are police on this case, you know. They will find out who killed Elissa. You didn't have to stay up half the night over at Dina's with Hannah."

I straightened up, feeling small bones in my back pop into place. I looked out the window again. "I wasn't there that long."

"But you didn't sleep." Pete reached out and traced gently under my eyes with his index finger. "That's obvious."

I made up my mind. "No, after I fought with Hannah, I went over and fought with Elissa's mom."

"You fought with her?" Pete's tone was incredulous.

I stole a look at him. "I thought maybe she knew something about the drug connection so I went over to see her."

Pete pulled his head back as though he were examining a new and curious discovery. "And did she?"

"She knew RJ was on drugs." My voice caught in my throat. "She said she wondered when I would figure it out. I'd thought she was my friend. If she knew, why didn't she tell me?"

"Is that what you fought about?"

"Actually, I didn't really do the fighting. I just felt so stunned. I couldn't believe it was happening. She was drunk-- and I'd never even seen her drink before. The house was filthy, and she's always been just an immaculate housekeeper, you know?"

Pete nodded.

"So I just kind of stood there, trying to absorb it all. She told me to get out--that I was harassing her. And she picked up a letter opener and looked like she was about to use it on me."

"She did what?"

I nodded, looking Pete square in the eyes. "She threatened me."

"Why?"

I shook my head as mystified as I'd been the night before. "She wanted me to get out."

"She wanted you out so she picked up a letter opener and threatened you," Pete repeated. "Has it occurred to you that this is not sane behavior?"

"I told you. She was drunk."

Pete took a sip of coffee and surveyed me over the mug. Finally he said, "That's pretty violent behavior. I don't think I should have to tell you that. That's your job. To me, that opens up a whole lot of questions."

I moved my hand in a circle, trying to spur him on. "Like?"

His blue eyes darkened. Slowly he said, "I don't want to encourage you in this amateur detective work you're doing. But what if it's not abnormal-- for Thea? What if she's prone to these drunken rages? Could she have killed Elissa?"

My breath caught in the back of my throat.

"She was there that day, wasn't she?" Pete prodded.

"She was at the rec center. I told you that, but...."

"But what? You don't think she could be that violent?"

The waitress bustled over and set up a stand for her tray with one hand, balancing the food with the other. The cinnamon roll smelled as good as it looked. The other plates overflowed with eggs, fried potatoes mixed with onions and covered with cheese, and thick slices of homemade bread.

She glanced around the table, frowning. "Should I put this back on the warmer until your son returns?" she asked, gesturing toward Josh's plate.

I shook my head, impatient with the interruption.

Pete waved toward the tray, smiling. "Don't worry about it. Josh had to leave, but I believe I can find room for his food."

The skin around the waitress's eyes crinkled as she smiled and set the cinnamon roll in front of me with a flourish. "I'll bet you can." She chuckled a bit as she set Josh's plate down in back of Pete's own omelet and fruit.

I waited until she was gone and Pete had his mouth full of omelet to say, "I can't believe you're sitting there so calmly, accusing Thea of killing her own daughter."

"Why shouldn't I be calm? Most murders are committed by someone the victim knows. You've been telling me it couldn't be RJ, and I want to believe you. So I have to look in the victim's circle of acquaintances. And now what you're telling me gives me reason to believe her mother has that capability."

I pinched off a piece of cinnamon bun, stuffed it in my mouth and swallowed it almost without chewing. "So this is just another investigation to you? Everything is not the way it looks."

"What? She didn't threaten you?" Pete reached across the table and held my arm, staring into my eyes. "Look, Kaye, you're a loyal friend, and I love you for it. But someone killed Elissa. If not RJ, then who?"

All right so maybe he wasn't being cold. He was just trying to be logical to help me. I popped a slice of Josh's potatoes in my mouth with my free hand. "I know someone killed her. But..."

"But don't let it be anyone you know and like."

I inched Josh's plate toward me and picked up another chunk of potato. I hadn't realized how hungry I was. And these were so good. "I didn't say that."

"Then you need to think like a cop and consider everyone a suspect," he said.

He was right of course, but I wasn't in the habit of scrutinizing my friends. Frowning, I ate more potato, noticing as I did that I'd worked my way through a good half of the plate.

Pete pushed Josh's plate across the table to me. "Do you like those? Have them."

I flushed and pushed the plate back at him. "I'm cutting all the fried food from my diet. Besides I thought you were going to eat this."

* * *

Pete left me off at home so he could catch up on some paperwork. I never even went back in the house, just jumped in the car and left. Josh lived not far from our house in a block full of beige and blue apartments. I walked quickly to get out of the cold, up the stairs to the weathered wood walkway outside the second story apartments. Even as I knocked on the peeling brown door, I could tell no one was home. I looked into the dusty picture window-- not caring if the neighbors from the all-too-close next building saw me.

The curtains were barely parted, leaving the front room in darkness. The best I could make out was the impression of a jumbled mound of blankets heaped on the couch. Disappointed, I stomped my cold feet and turned toward the car.

"Hi, you looking for Josh?"

Startled, I reared back a bit. It was the little brunette from church, practically waving her hand in my face. What was her name? Tina? No, Tiffany.

"Sort of," I answered.

"He's probably visiting his mom in the hospital."

Ooh. That made me feel lower than the cellar floor. I'd just been hassling some poor kid whose mom was in the hospital? "I didn't know."

Tiffany nodded, her solemn expression sitting oddly on her bright young face. "Yeah, it sucks, doesn't it? They thought the chemo was helping and that maybe she would get better. Then, bam!" She clapped her hands together. "There she goes again."

Remission like cancer? I put my ice-cold hands in my coat pockets and stared. "Yeah," I said absently. "It does suck."

I climbed into the car, feeling my lack of sleep. Taking a thoughtful sip of the coffee I'd brought with me from the restaurant, I switched on the heater to warm up my always icy feet.

Suddenly a couple of things made sense. Like how someone I'd thought was an involved parent could be unaware that her teenage son spent the night at my unsupervised house. Like why my daughter was so protective of Josh.

And the drug connection between Josh and Flynn when Hannah said Josh hated Flynn. Was Josh trying to help his mom by getting her marijuana to help with the nausea caused by chemotherapy? Medical marijuana was legal now in Colorado, but I'd heard that it was still difficult to obtain. That would explain his saying that his mom knew where he was. Or was that too much of a leap?

Decisively, I started the car and headed back to Dina's. I was going to get my answers whether Hannah liked it or not.

* * *

But no one responded to my knock at Dina's house. I couldn't even look in her window. Her thick white curtains were closely drawn. Thoughts churning, I headed back to the car. Of course, Hannah had probably gone to church herself this morning. She did go most Sundays. And Dina and Phil were adults. They didn't need my permission to go out.

So now what? I felt as unsettled as I had the night before. Tapping my hand restlessly against the steering wheel, I decided to visit Brenda's. Maybe Zack knew more than he'd told me--or the police--before.

Brenda lived in one of the pricey new developments that had sprung up on the northwest side of town. A huge brick wall encased adobe style houses with the requisite red tile roofing and three car garages. In an effort to curb my jealousy, I looked for something to criticize in the houses and found nothing. Each house had its own distinct personality, the yards were spacious, and the windows huge, ensuring that the interiors were filled with light. The contrast with my own house couldn't have been clearer. I was certifiably green-eyed, and I hadn't been born that way. Danielle answered the door, dressed in an open pink terry bathrobe over top of a pink and white night gown. Her bare feet, toes painted a bright, sparkly blue, peeked out from beneath it all. The house behind her seemed suitably Sunday morning quiet. She surveyed me anxiously, her expression easing only slightly when she recognized me.

"Hi, Danielle. How are you doing?"

She stuck her finger in her mouth, something I'd never seen her do before. What was she now? First grade, wasn't it? "Is your mom home?" I asked.

She nodded.

"Can I speak to her?"

Without moving from the door or taking her finger from her mouth, Danielle bellowed, "Mom!"

If Brenda hadn't been awake before, she was now. I stole a glance at my watch. Luckily it was pushing noon.

Brenda scurried down the curving stairs. Travis trailed after her.

"Kaye! Come in, come in," she said breathlessly. "Danielle, you let Kaye in and get her something to drink. What are you doing, standing there, making her wait outside the door in the cold?"

I crinkled my nose at Danielle and smiled.

She took my hand, tugging me into the white tiled entryway. Looking up into my eyes, her dark eyes shadowed, she said softly, "I'm going to be the oldest when Zack goes to jail."

I looked quickly from Brenda to Danielle. God, what could I say? I wanted to tell Danielle something soothing, make it all better. But this was not a fear that could be smoothed away. I squatted down and looked

Danielle in the eyes, so close I could smell the sugary cereal on her breath. "This is all pretty scary, huh?"

She nodded and put her finger back in her mouth, swaying from one foot to the other as she regarded me with wide eyes.

Keeping my eyes on hers, I reached out to touch her arm. "You know, don't you, that no matter where he is, Zack will always be your older brother? You can still talk to him, you know."

"It won't be the same, though." Danielle took her finger from her mouth and turned away, a tear sliding silently down her face.

I looked up at Brenda, unable to keep my dismay from my face. She touched Danielle's shoulder lightly. Danielle looked up, her shoulders shaking with sobs.

Brenda hugged her and said softly, "You don't worry about that right now, you hear?"

Danielle nodded, but the tears kept coming.

"I mean it now," Brenda chided her. "We don't know what's going to happen yet."

Danielle's head bobbed again.

"Okay, now." Brenda's tone was firm. That subject was finished. "You and Travis go on upstairs and get dressed. You can't go around in your pj's all day, can you?"

I stood up, flexing aching knees. "I'm sorry," I said quietly, meeting her eyes. "This must all be pretty hard."

She shrugged, her eyes avoiding mine. I saw the glitter of tears though.

"No harder on me than on you," she said.

I nodded and took a deep breath. "I wanted to talk to you and Zack. I'd hoped maybe if we go back over this a bit, we could figure out something that would help."

She shooed me gently toward the elegant blue and white living room. "You're welcome to stay. But I have to say, that lawyer I got last night, he said don't talk to nobody about this."

I moved toward the huge white brocade sofa, and sank into the soft cushions. From there, my footprints were noticeable in the thick blue carpet.

Brenda perched tentatively on the chair across from me, her sneakered foot tapping. "Can I get you something to drink?"

"No, that's fine." I rose to leave. "You're probably right. It probably wasn't a good idea anyway."

Brenda stopped me with an outstretched arm. "I didn't say I thought it was a bad idea. I told you the lawyer said we shouldn't talk about it. He said the boys had two separate cases, and that we should keep it that way."

I sank back into the cushions.

Brenda's voice became softer, closer to tears again. "I don't want to just defend Zack. I've got to know what happened. 'Cause if he did it, I want to know. I want him punished. 'Cause that's not the way I raised him."

Before I could say anything, blurt out any well-meaning but meaningless, comforting phrases, she'd fled the room, calling for Zack as she went. In less than five minutes, she was back with two steaming mugs and Zack, dressed in baggy jeans and a long-sleeved tee that said "Property of the FBI".

I shook my head and smiled at Brenda, waving at the mug. "Hey, I told you not to bother."

She strode quickly across the room and handed me the mug. "No bother. I know how you like your coffee."

Actually, I'd had more than enough coffee to make my hands shake all day, but I took the mug and thanked her before turning to Zack. "So how are you doing?"

He shrugged, leaning against the door with his arms crossed. His scowl told the story, but he said, "Okay, I guess. Where's RJ?"

An almost physical pain stabbed me as I remembered where RJ was, but I tried to keep the feeling from showing in my face. "That's one of the things I'd like to talk to you about."

"Zack, get in here and sit down," said his mother. "I already told you. We both want to talk to you."

Zack shrugged and looked at me with narrowed eyes, but he slouched into the room and flung himself on the footstool by his mother's chair. "So where's RJ?" he asked again, dark eyes on me.

I lifted my chin and took a deep breath. "I sent him to an in-patient drug program. I wanted him to get help."

Brenda's eyes widened and she turned quickly to her son.

Though I studied Zack's face, I saw no sign of surprise. "How about you, Zack? Are you using?"

Zack shook his head, flattening his face into a look of patience. "I don't have the time or the money for that junk."

"But you knew RJ was using?"

He hunched a shoulder, deliberately looking away from me. "Yeah, I knew."

Had everyone known? My voice hard, I said, "And you didn't want to say something to me?"

"Wasn't any of my business. Besides why should I tell you anything?"

Brenda leaned forward on her chair and tilted her son's chin up, speaking directly into his face. "You be respectful."

He jerked his head away, his lower lip extended, his eyes narrowed again. But after a quick look at his mother's face, he replaced it with a slight smile and a polite lift to his eyebrows. His shrug belied his next word. "Sorry."

I stared at him with the same sensation I'd had when I looked at RJ at the police station. I'd thought I knew this kid. Obviously, I didn't.

"And what about Elissa? Did you know about her, too?" I asked softly.

He smirked. "Everybody knew 'bout that ho."

My heart sped up, then stopped, before plodding heavily on. "What did you call her?"

His face held nothing now but a wish to be helpful. "A ho. You know a slut."

I shook my head in wonder.

A look of impatience for adult stupidity crossed his face, but he quickly covered it. "Like she sold it to whoever could give her enough for the next high."

"You're saying she was a prostitute?"

"She didn't go out and sell it on East Colfax, if that's what you mean," he said. "But everybody knew. She used that field to screw."

"Yeah, well, she must have taken a vacation in the winter time then," Brenda said, her mouth pulled up to one side. "Otherwise she'd have froze her hind end off in the snow."

Zack laughed. "She had other places, too. One guy told me he did her on her parents' bed." He shook his head, genuinely amused. "Not that they knew that, of course."

"Of course," I echoed, horrified.

But Thea did know about the drugs. And she knew about Elissa's partying and running away. She even knew about RJ.

"Elissa's mom is a b-i-t...." He bit off the end of the word.

Following his gaze, I saw Brenda, brows lowered, and mouth a straight line.

Then he shrugged, good-naturedly. "I won't say it if you don't want me to. But everybody knew. Elissa told everybody about her mother. She'd come into school with her hair half pulled out and a big old red hand print on her face."

Sharply, I said, "I used to live next door to them, and I never saw anything like that."

Zack smiled slowly, a smile that suggested that I'd never seen RJ's problem either. I wanted to lean forward and slap him--the oddest feeling considering I'd spent my life working against violence. My face grew hot. Breathing hard, I let the feeling blaze out of my eyes. But I said only, "Her mother knew more than you knew. She told me about the drugs. She even tried to get Elissa help."

"Elissa said her mom knew about the drugs but after that last counseling thing, 'lissa laid it on the line. She wasn't going back for none of that. She told her Mom, 'You try and make me, and I'll tell Dad that you're still drinking.'"

So the drinking wasn't just a reaction to Elissa's death? Worse yet, Thea had let Elissa control the situation and keep doing drugs to keep Thea's own secret safe. No wonder the counseling didn't work. And George still didn't know?

I'd thought Thea loved her daughter more than anything. She'd seemed like such a wonderful mother. The whole thing left a bitter taste in my mouth. Yet.... "I can't believe that if Elissa was sleeping around that Thea wouldn't know--and stop it."

But maybe Thea did finally find out about Elissa's promiscuity. Maybe Thea had stopped her.

When I left Brenda's, the sky had clouded over again and a sharp wind gusted right through my heavy coat. I drove home, miserably tired and numb, Zack's voice echoing through my brain. "Everybody knew 'bout that ho."

The house was silent except for the hum of the furnace and the howl of the wind. Although it wasn't quite three yet, the cloudy sky made it look later in the day. The house was gloomy enough to need lights turned on, but I didn't. I flopped down on the couch, my legs extended in front of me. I had nothing left. No energy, no feeling. I couldn't think. All I wanted was sleep.

When the phone rang, I was already half way there. "Hello," I said groggily.

"I'd like to speak to Ms. Kaye Berreano."

The voice sounded vaguely familiar. I shook my head. Probably a sales call. "You are," I said baldly making no attempt to keep my tone polite.

"Ms Berreano, this is Lena McQuire from Bright Harvest Behavioral Health service. How are you tonight?"

Bright Harvest--the drug treatment center. Lena. Okay, I was awake now. I forced my voice to be affable. "I'm doing okay. How about you?"

"Ms Berreano, I'm calling tonight about RJ. I'm afraid, I have some unpleasant news."

"Yes?"

"Ms Berreano, I want you to know that we take the utmost precautions at Bright Harvest. New admits are given no privileges whatsoever."

She'd explained this before. No visits from parents, no phones. I'd gotten it. "Uh huh."

"I just wanted to stress that. All our residents are asked to give up their shoes and their coats when they first come in. But even so, these things happen."

So get to the point already. I sat up on the couch. "What things happen?"

"Ms. Berreano, I'm afraid that your son has run away."

Chapter 16

My mouth felt suddenly dry. I swallowed hard to try to ease it, succeeding only in making my tight throat feel tighter. I felt as though I were choking. Breathing fast, I blurted out the first thing that came to mind. "So RJ is somewhere outside in the snow and cold with no coat or shoes."

"We were hoping that perhaps he'd come home."

"He hasn't--and he hasn't called. So he's out there with nothing."

"Sometimes these kids get shoes from other kids."

I ran a hand through my hair. "So are you telling me some other kid loaned mine his shoes so RJ could run away and you didn't notice?"

"Sometimes loaned is a, shall we say, flexible, word."

"You're saying RJ stole the shoes?"

"That's what the other kid claims."

Was that supposed to be reassuring? "How could you let him do this?"

"This is one of those areas where kids need to assume responsibility, and you have to let them. We're not a locked facility. So if kids want to go--they can go. We can't stop them. As for letting him steal the shoes, I don't think you should assume that someone saw him take them and said nothing. He did that, as he walked out, on his own."

"But someone was supposed to be watching."

"We can hardly watch every kid every moment. These kids have to want to be here and want to get help."

How Bright Harvest could expect kids to take responsibility when the staff there took none was beyond me. I blew hard out of pursed lips. "So he has shoes, but no coat. Now what happens?"

"We've made the phone call to the police to report him as a runaway. They'll be on the lookout for him here in Denver. You might want to report him as a runaway in Arvada and make sure they know what's going on. That seems a likely place for him to head for. Of course he could also head for his Dad's house and you might want to notify police there also."

"And just what will you do?"

She gave a long sigh, and the line was silent a moment as though she were collecting her thoughts. "We've searched the premises and the immediate area--and notified the police. There's not much more we can do. When you find RJ, we can have a meeting to decide if it's appropriate to readmit him to the treatment facility."

"When I find RJ? So you guys are giving up on him? Aren't you the one who told me the other day that you felt certain that RJ exhibited signs of drug use?"

"You can call his friends--"

I couldn't believe this. "So it's just up to me. We sent him to you for help." She didn't say anything. "Tell me why I would want to readmit him to some place that took no responsibility for keeping him there in the first place?"

Lena's voice showed her heart. "I'm sorry. But we've really done all we could. These kids have to want treatment before we can help them."

I heard a deep breath on the other end of the wire.

Then in a more upbeat voice, she said, "So if you've decided you don't want your son to return, you could come and pick up his things any day during our normal office hours."

I could almost hear her thinking, "End of case". I knew how it was from her angle too. Bright Harvest was a for-profit operation. There were plenty of kids with drug problems. Bright Harvest didn't have to spin their wheels with the hard cases. Bottom line? It wasn't about kids. It was about money. I hung up feeling desperately alone.

I called Roger first--but had no more luck getting him than Bright Harvest had. I left a message. When I called the Arvada police, the dispatcher wanted me to come in and file a runaway report.

"I believe one has been filed in the city of Denver."

"Ma'am, you don't need to file in every municipality. If your son ran away in the city of Denver, Denver will put it on the computer nationally."

I sighed, trying to restrain myself. "Look, the drug rehabilitation center he ran away from told me to call. They think it seems probable that RJ will head back toward home, and I'd like to make sure that the Arvada police are looking for him."

Her sigh seemed louder than mine. "Okay, I'll see to it that our officers are informed."

Yeah, but would anyone really be on the lookout for him? I bit my tongue to keep myself from asking that, and went on to call his friends. I didn't bother with Zack. A quick mental calculation reminded me that I'd called Bright Harvest this morning. RJ must have been there then. And later, I was at Zack's when RJ must have been on the run. Wherever RJ was, it wasn't Zack's. The problem was none of his other friends professed to know anything about where RJ might be either.

Without even spending time debating with myself, I found myself back in the car heading to Dina's. If anyone knew where RJ was, Hannah would.

No matter what our differences, I knew she would help. And I needed to be with one of my kids.

Snowflakes swirled in the wind as I approached Dina's little brick ranch. Unlike earlier in the day, I could tell someone was there. The heavy white curtains had been pulled back and the flicker of the TV set came through the curtain sheers. The sweet smell of bread baking wafted in the air by the front door.

Hannah answered the door, dressed all in black--jeans, T- shirt, and shoes. I could tell from the tilt of her chin that she still had an attitude. In her hand was a bottle of black nail polish.

Evidently, I'd interrupted her, not that I was sorry. "Depressed are we, Hannah?"

She rolled her eyes. "Now what, Mother?"

"I want to talk to you."

"We've already been through all this." She moved to shut the door.

I put my hand out to block it. "No." I looked firmly in her blue eyes. "Not quite. We need to talk."

"Hannah, who's at the door?" Dina's voice sounded sleepy. Soft thuds from the vicinity of the bedroom made me wonder if she'd been lying down.

I hoped I hadn't wakened her up. I poked my head around the door to look. Hannah fell back a step as though to avoid contact with me. The hall was dark, and the bedroom door was a darker shadow to the side. Dina emerged from the darkness. She rubbed the sleep from her eyes.

"It's just me, Dina," I said. "I came over to talk to Hannah again."

Dina spread her arms in welcome. "Come on in. It's cold out there."

I nodded and stepped in, pulling the door shut behind me. Hannah shook her head, her mouth puckered as though she swallowed something sour. Something about the look on her face--the trembling lower lip, reminded me of when she was about two and wanted to cry. Attitude or not, she was still my baby. I reached out to smooth her hair. "Hannah, the whole problem was, I had a rule, and you deliberately defied it. What do you think I should do when that happens?"

Her whole body stiff as though she couldn't tolerate my touch, she retorted. "Get rid of the rule."

I lifted an eyebrow. "Get real."

"It's messed up. I need time to study with Josh."

"Until five in the morning?"

She shrugged. "There was a big test the next day, and Josh was behind. And then..."

"Yes?"

Her nostrils flared and she tossed her head, effectively shrugging off my hand. "Nothing! We fell asleep. Why don't you trust me?"

"You know, guys have been known to take advantage of girls in these kind of situations."

Dina scrunched her nose at me.

Hannah sighed heavily, and glanced at Dina as if to say, see what I have to put up with? "Mother!"

Okay so it wasn't diplomatic of me. "I'm sure Josh is perfectly fine, Hannah, but I don't know him very well."

"You know him well enough to yell at him and treat me like a child in front of him. I'm too old to be sent to my room."

"Your father started that. I was just following through," I said defensively.

It was a thin argument, and Hannah knew that as well as I. "Since when do you do what Dad wants?"

"Hannah, we can't keep doing this. I miss you and I want you home. But I need to be able to depend on you to do what you're supposed to."

She shrugged away from me, slinking back against the wall and trying to hide her face with hair. There, blinking back tears, she said in a shaky voice, "If you really missed me, none of this would have happened."

I stepped forward and put my arms firmly around her, hugging her hard. "You don't think I missed you?"

She shrugged, a stiff and awkward movement in my arms. She didn't look up. With my finger, I tilted her chin up, making her look at me again. "I missed you," I said.

"Of course she did, Hannah! Wait until you have kids," Dina said.

Hannah groaned, and sniffed, at the same time, snuggling into my arms like a toddler. Her voice muffled by her head's position lodged firmly against my shoulder, she said, "That's what Mom's worried about. Don't you know?"

She wasn't pulling any punches. Well, neither would I. "You're right. I'm afraid of pregnancy, and AIDS, and STD'S, and..."

At that she threw her head up to stare at me, blue eyes wide and hard, her mouth an OH of outrage. "Mother! You have to trust me to be grown up. I'm fifteen now. I can take care of myself."

"And you do." I smiled at her and pulled her back against my shoulder to stroke her hair. "But I've learned a couple of things by getting to be old enough to be your mother, and frankly I don't see the point in putting temptation in your way. When two people spend a lot of time alone together, they're bound to start... well, thinking about sex at least."

Hannah shrugged. "We thought about that stuff a long time ago, Mom. It's not that."

I nodded, and said softly, "I know. I went to Josh's. Why didn't you tell me about his mom?"

Hannah eased her shoulders back away from me, bracing her arms between us. Her eyes flicked across my face, evaluating. "His mom doesn't want people to know how sick she is. She doesn't want anyone making a fuss."

Softly, not wanting to disturb this tenuous cease-fire, I said, "And Josh doesn't want anyone knowing he's buying marijuana to help his mom over the chemo."

Hannah bit her lip, a small wrinkle appearing in her forehead. "How did you know?"

I shook my head. "I didn't really. I just put bits and pieces together with what's been going on. And I realized why my generous and responsible daughter was condoning things that she knew were wrong."

Hannah dropped her eyes, and hunched one shoulder. "I knew that Josh shouldn't be there when you weren't. But a couple of times, his mom got sick all of a sudden and had to go to the hospital. He just needed to be with someone. And he didn't know where to go."

I nodded. "I figured that out finally. You and I are going to have to work out some sort of solution."

"Like what?"

It was my turn to shrug. "Maybe I need to get a job with no night shifts."

"But your job is important to you..."

I shook my head at her. "Not as important as my daughter."

Dina cleared her throat. "Come on, you two. You can't solve all of the world's problems standing in the hallway. Come on in and get some dinner."

I shook my head at her. "I can't. There's something else I have to tell Hannah and then I'm hoping..."

Dina took my arm and shook her head back at me. "Whatever it is you can tell us over dinner. I've got homemade vegetable soup and fresh baked bread with some Camembert cheese. It's all ready, and I'm not taking no for an answer."

I shook my head, speechless and near to tears. I needed to find RJ. And I needed to tell Hannah so she could help me.

Hannah jiggled my arm. "Mom, what's the matter?"

I sniffed and tried to smile. Who was the mother here after all?

With an air of earnestness, she said, "I'll eat quick. Really. And you can talk while you eat. But it's like Grandmom always says. Everything looks a little better after a rest and a good meal."

"Dina, really, I appreciate everything you've done. But I can..."

"Phil," Dina called. "Come out here and tell Kaye to eat with us."

Obediently, Dina's husband Phil lumbered from the bedroom wearing only a pair of gray sweat pants and carrying their one-year-old son nestled sleepily next to his bare chest. He shook his head, the shaggy fringe of hair around his bald spot flopping with the movement. "You know you have to do what boss lady here says, Kaye."

"I can't. I've..."

Both Phil's and the baby's heads disappeared beneath a red T-shirt as Phil tried to dress around the drowsy little one.

Dina answered me, "Of course you can. You have to. We need to finish figuring out about Thanksgiving next week, too." Dina put an arm around my shoulder and steered me into their dining room. "You're going to bring Pete to Thanksgiving with you, right?"

When we reached the table, Dina pulled out a chair and pushed me gently into it. I perched on it gingerly, afraid to lean on their glass dining table and mar its sparkle with my handprints. Dina nodded her satisfaction and disappeared into the kitchen only to emerge a minute later with a steaming crock of soup. She ladled soup and cut bread as I brought them all up to speed on what had been happening. The soup was warming, the bread delicious. But I sat through dinner on the edge of my chair, feeling like I should be doing something about RJ.

"What else can you do, Kaye?" Dina asked. "You've called the police and his friends."

I glanced over at Hannah, "I'd hoped that Hannah would have some ideas."

She'd been quiet ever since she'd heard me say that RJ had run away. Now she sat with her head bent, playing with some vegetables left in her soup bowl.

I took a deep breath and said, "If not, maybe I can drive around the area of Bright Harvest, see if I can spot him."

Hannah looked up, her expression a mixture of pity and teen exasperation toward a none too bright parent. "Mom, he's not dumb. He knows how to use a bus. He's gone."

"Hannah, what else can I do? None of his friends know where he is. A couple of them are so concerned they asked me to tell him to call if he turns up."

Hannah shook her head, smiling a closed mouth smile that looked so sad. "Mom, they're not going to tell you if they know where he is. They're on his side. Did you ask Zack's mom?"

"Honey, I was over there when RJ ran. He's not there."

She raised her eyebrows.

"What does that mean? You think Zack could hide him? I was there at Zack's house."

"Zack is..." She shrugged and looked beyond me, lost in her thoughts. "I wouldn't trust Zack," she finally finished.

I'd figured that out for myself this morning. But still, Zack was younger than RJ and a little easier to assess--now that I knew what to look for. I blurted out my real worry. "I was wondering about Flynn."

"Flynn?"

"Well, that's where RJ's getting the drugs, isn't it?"

Hannah just looked at me and shook her head.

Despite her protests, when we were done eating, she went with me to search for RJ. We drove all over, through the rapidly worsening snow. From time to time, Hannah would point out places where kids hung out. Every time I saw a lanky young figure in baggy jeans, shoulders hunched against the driving snow, my heart stopped. But it was never RJ.

I wanted my son so badly, I was screaming inside--calling out to him from my soul, my heart. I heard no answer.

Finally, we went home, where I looked hopefully for signs of his presence. I checked it from top to bottom, but my house was exactly as I left it.

Hannah lugged her backpack full of clothes to her room, but hesitated outside it. "I'm sorry, Mom."

I shook my head. "For what?"

She sat the pack down carefully and came over and hugged me, eyes brimming. "I should have told you sooner about RJ. And Josh. And I should have listened."

I shook my head again, my own eyes prickling with tears. "RJ isn't your fault."

"I could have told you when I knew about the drugs. Then maybe none of this would have happened."

None of what would have happened? He probably would still have run away from rehab. Or was she saying...? My heart skipped a beat and I felt as though I had to breathe faster to try to catch up. "Hannah, are you saying you think RJ killed Elissa?"

She hesitated a moment then shook her head, eyes downcast. She might as well have screamed her doubts in my ears. The effect was as deafening.

* * *

The wind howled outside, throwing snow against the windows. Unable to sleep again I decided to wash RJ's dirty clothes and clean his room. I don't know what I was hoping for--a note that said he didn't kill Elissa but knew who did? A notice from the doctor giving him a clean urine analysis? Maybe just a connection with this kid--this son--this teenager of mine. I didn't deny to myself that I was looking for a clue to where he might be now.

I didn't get any of it. No alibi for the murder of an old friend and neighbor--no reprieve from the reality of his drug abuse. I couldn't find the son I knew in that room, and it didn't hold any clues telling me where else to look. But then, I could have found just about anything else I might have wanted. The room was a mess. The pipe full of ash was still outside his window as it had been the night he left. Clothes were piled knee-deep. Plates with congealed spaghetti and frozen burrito wrappers lay scattered on top. A bottle of correction fluid had spilled under his bed--ruining the carpet. A small plastic bag full of marijuana was stuffed in the pocket of a pair of jeans nearby. But there were no notes, unless I counted the ones from his teachers scrawled on the top of his school papers which lay scattered around the room: Late assignment, they said or incomplete. One, compressed into a ball and stuffed into the corner of his closet said in huge red letters, "This is unacceptable. Please see me after class."

Finally, after I'd gotten the bed stripped, the clothes washed and neatly folded at its foot, and two huge full trash bags on the carpet by the door, I slumped down on the bed holding the marijuana and let the tears roll down my face.

I should have known. I should have paid attention. I stared around the room at the posters. They should have been my first clues. A tall skinny guy, his face painted like a clown and his hair an improbable red Mohawk, leered down at me from one. Fire? The poster posed the question in blazing letters. What the heck did that mean?

Another in neon ice-shadowed letters that twisted in triplicate over themselves, making reading difficult, might have said think. It might as easily have said drunk. Was it any clearer under the black light? I shook my head. I went into the bathroom and flushed the contents of the bag. Then I went back into the bedroom and cried.

"Mom?" Hannah bent over me, shaking my shoulder, a crease lining her forehead. She was dressed for school. Sunlight streamed in from the window behind her. "You okay?"

Why wouldn't I be okay? I blinked up at her. My legs and back ached from being curled in a tiny spot on RJ's narrow bed, and my eyes burned and felt glued shut from all the crying I'd done. And I'd spent part of the night considering whether the kids wouldn't be better off under Roger's custody. But I wasn't going to say any of that to her. I sat up abruptly, almost bumping heads with her. "I'm fine."

"Okay," she said, but her face still held a question. "I'm going to school now."

I consulted my watch. 7:30. School. And work. Like any normal day. As though anything could be normal. But I nodded and stood up to kiss her. "Have a good day, honey."

"Are you sure you're all right?"

"I'm fine, Hannah. Go!"

She practically backed out of the room, watching me with eyes wide and biting her lower lip. I pushed the hair away from my face, trying to smile at her, wanting to ease her worry. She could probably see the signs of my rough night on my face. After all, I didn't usually sleep in one of the kids' rooms. I would have to work harder at getting things back to normal for her. She didn't deserve all this turmoil. "It's okay, Hannah. Really. Have a good day, honey."

Finally, she smiled. "You, too, Mom."

I stayed in bed until I heard her let herself out then I stood up and debated going to work. I just wanted to stay home and watch for RJ. But I knew I had to go. For one thing, it was time to earn my pay and confront Flynn. I'd known for days that he was dealing drugs, and had waited to hear what Josh's side of the matter was. But it had to be dealt with--along with the rest of my suspicions.

I bundled up and went out to scrape the snow off the car. The blowing snow that made the world into a bleak white landscape.

My heart had an almost physical ache. No longer able to shed tears outwardly, I was crying on the inside--worrying about where RJ was and how he was surviving in this horrible weather.

A half hour later, I barely got the heavy oak door closed against the arctic wind bellowing outside the safe house, when Flynn appeared in the entryway. Dressed in his usual black overcoat and black jeans, he looked grungy and slimy. He had the nerve to laugh right in my face. "I hear RJ busted himself out from that place you stuck him in."

I wanted to grab the little jerk's black clad shoulders, not caring about the grunge, and shake him until his brains rattled in that thick skull of his. Instead I contented myself with getting right into his unwashed face, and saying through clenched teeth. "What do you know about RJ?"

Anita scurried over, her face as red as her dress. "What is the matter with you, Kaye? Is there a problem?"

Liz leaned against the office doorframe, watching silently.

I tried to pull myself together. "Yes, Anita." I breathed heavily, toe to toe with Flynn. "There is a problem." Reluctantly turning away from her son, I pivoted to face Anita and Liz. "It has been brought forcibly to my attention that Flynn has been involved with selling drugs, and we don't allow that in this house."

Anita's face turned even redder, and she sputtered, "I won't stay in a place where they make unfounded accusations like..."

Liz waved her to be silent. "Is this unfounded, Kaye?"

"No," I took a deep breath and swallowed. "It is not. On my way home from work a few days ago, I witnessed Flynn in what looked like a drug transaction outside of Lawrence elementary school. I knew the other boy also. I didn't say anything, because I wanted to be sure of my facts. But I've spoken to other parties concerned with this, and at this point, I feel I have substantiated my facts to the point where I would feel comfortable presenting all of this to the police."

"Like Josh is going to tell the police he bought pot from me for his mama," Flynn sneered.

Liz's eyes narrowed.

Anita's mouth fell open, and she put her hand to her mouth. "Do you know what you just said? Do you even realize?"

She flew across the room to Flynn, her face red enough to make me worry about a stroke, then grabbed his shoulders and gave him the shaking I'd hoped to do. "I can't believe you. I can't believe after all we've gone through that you could stand there and calmly admit to selling drugs. Don't we have enough to deal with? Isn't life hard enough for you right now? What is the matter with you?"

Flynn put his hands up to ward off his mother, looking as startled at the attack as though his pet bird had bitten him. I didn't know she had it in her. If only her husband could see her like this. I moved to pull Anita off.

Liz shook her head at me, and said, "I must say, Flynn, I was just about to tell Kaye that I needed more proof, but it seems you've taken care of that yourself."

Flynn grabbed his mother's wrists, struggling to hold her away from him. With his lower lip curled, and his face darkened, he said, "What the hell is that matter with you? I didn't admit anything."

Anita squirmed away from him and stood breathing hard, hands on her hips. "What, so now you're so stoned yourself you don't know what you're saying? Kaye never mentioned any boy's name, son! She never said what you sold him either! You're the one who said that. That's enough for me. I'll call the cops myself."

"Yeah, and what will you tell them? You heard I sold some guy medical marijuana for his mother? It's legal here in Colorado. Josh's mom has a medical certificate."

"Uh huh, and you're a licensed provider. What about Elissa? Did you sell to her?" I asked.

"You don't know what you're talking about," Flynn said.

"Your girlfriend, Elissa Pappas. The one who was murdered," I said heavily.

"I didn't sell her jack. And you can't prove I did. Besides she was getting off drugs. She'd promised her mom."

Anita said, "If you're dealing, it won't be hard to prove. I'll give them permission. They can search your..."

Flynn laughed. "They can search wherever the hell they want. They won't find shit."

Anita balled her hands into fists, and got right into his face, standing on her tiptoes to do it. She spoke in a calm and quiet voice that would have chilled me to the bone if I'd been him. "All right, they won't find anything. But you've already told me all I need to know. And I'll tell you straight, your father might be a drunk and a wife beater, but he won't hold with drugs either. You're going straight into rehab. And I know he'll support me in that."

Flynn looked down his nose, a smile curling his lips. "Like you can make me. Ask her." He pointed at me. "Rehab didn't work so well for her precious son."

Anita stepped back and looked to see where he was pointing.

I nodded and looked him squarely in the face. "It's true. RJ ran away from rehab last night. What do you know about that?"

Behind me, I heard Liz murmur, "Oh, God, Kaye. I'm sorry."

Flynn shrugged. "I don't know jack."

Anita stepped forward, pounding him on the chest. "You already told her you knew he was gone. You know something. Tell her."

Eyebrows kinked, Flynn fended off his mother yet again, shaking his head. "Stop it. All right." His breath came hard, and he never took his wide eyes from his mother. "All I know is Wendy Mattison called me last night to tell me RJ was gone. I think she heard it from her." He waved toward me.

Wendy Mattison? A name from RJ's address book--I couldn't even put a face to her. "Yes, I did call her last night," I said slowly. "So you don't know where he is?"

With his mother still in his face, glaring in his eyes, Flynn finally appeared almost cowed. "No, I don't know," he muttered.

"And what about Elissa?" I asked again.

He stepped forward, brows lowered, teeth visibly clenched. "What the hell are you saying? Are you asking if I killed my own girlfriend? Is that it?"

I stood my ground, aware of Anita now watching with frightened eyes. I knew the feeling--the punch in the gut doubt of your own kid. "That's what I'm asking, yes."

"Seems to me," Flynn drawled. "RJ's the one they've been questioning about that. Isn't that so?"

I heard Liz's quick intake of breath, and wished I talked to her about all this. Still, now was not the time to hesitate. I didn't want this punk to think he intimidated me.

"Seems to me," I imitated his tone, "you know an awful lot about it. Including everything about RJ's backpack. How would you know it was RJ's? That was never in the paper. Could it be that you're the one who borrowed it?"

Anita looked from Flynn to me obviously trying to understand what we were talking about--and decide whom to believe.

"Elissa had RJ's backpack as a joke. She bragged to me about it. But she wasn't laughing in the end, was she? You let that little faggot son of yours near me, I'll kill him myself for what he did to her."

Chapter 17

"**Y**ou're not going to be doing anything to anyone," Anita shouted in Flynn's face. "Do you hear me?"

"Kaye, telephone." Dina's voice came from just behind me. She'd entered the room so quietly, I hadn't heard her.

"Not right now," I tossed over my shoulder. I had to make eye contact with Flynn. I had to. I had to know. Did he really think RJ killed Elissa?

"I think you'd better, Kaye." Dina's voice was firm.

Reluctantly, I turned. Her white face and thin lips told me this was bad news. "It's Roger," she mouthed.

Of course it was. His timing always did suck. Oh, I'd talk to him all right. But he wouldn't like it. I took a deep breath and nodded, head down, already moving toward the door.

The office was a confusing morass of papers spread judiciously throughout, pretty much obscuring the gray metal desks. I carefully moved stacks of forms off a secretarial chair to the top of a small file cabinet. Then pivoting to hit the chair just right to avoid toppling onto the floor, I sat, trying to collect my thoughts in the quiet before picking up the phone.

The office was cold, I felt it even through my coat, which I had yet to take off, but Roger's voice was colder. "Don't you think you could have had the courtesy to give me this kind of news in person? At the very least, you could have waited until you had me on the phone. But to just leave this kind of message on my machine smacks of the most..."

I didn't have the time for this garbage. "Are you concerned about our son or your feelings?" I cut in.

"Of course I'm concerned about our son, but..."

"That's what I assumed. So I left the message so you could start looking for him, too."

"At the very least, you could have been available to answer my questions. As it was, I got a busy signal at your place for hours, followed by no answer--well into the night."

"You could have called Bright Harvest. They were the ones with the answers and..."

I wasn't the only one who could interrupt. Roger overrode my voice. "Well, I did, and they told me that you'd withdrawn him."

Speaking loudly so he could hear me over his own meanderings, I said, "I spent the night trying to contact his friends--seeing who might know where he was. Then I drove around with Hannah to see if I could spot him. Any objections?"

"You kept Hannah out on a school night?"

I sighed. Why did I even ask? Of course he had objections--probably in triplicate. Not that he wasn't right about the late hours on a school night I thought, with a pang of guilt. "I asked for Hannah's help and she gave it--willingly. She went to school on time today."

"Did you find him?" Finally Roger spoke in a calmer voice.

"No."

"And you signed him out of the program?"

"I haven't done it yet, but I will when I go to pick up his things. I can't believe these people. They took no responsibility whatsoever for his leaving. Aren't you the least bit angry over that?"

"Of course I'm angry. But withdrawing him from the program..."

"We'll find another program--one which can take responsibility."

"Oh ho, so now Ms. Counselor is going to bring her expertise to the problem. Did it occur to you that I might have some say so in this matter?"

"Since I seem to have to do all of this by myself--I decided to make the decisions. Where were you last night when I needed you? When RJ needed you? This isn't the first time you were missing in action." Without wasting time waiting for his answer, I went on. "Do you know what a jerk you are?"

"Yes, I do," he said.

"What?"

"I know that sometimes I can be a jerk," he repeated patiently.

I laughed and shook my head, brushing away tears of anger and hurt. "That is your one redeeming quality."

"I'm sorry." Roger's voice was now so low, I was tempted to turn up the volume on the phone. "How did we get here, Kaye? I never wanted a divorce--let alone a kid on drugs and suspected of murder. Did we do this to him?"

If he hadn't wanted a divorce, he shouldn't have played around. But that was water halfway to the reservoir by now. Besides, I knew what he meant. "Yeah, I know. After I got home last night, I spent the night cleaning RJ's room, wondering where I went wrong."

He cleared his throat, and emitted a strangled chuckle. "You and your cleaning."

He sounded pretty choked up. His other redeeming quality was that he really did care about our kids. After twenty years of marriage, I knew what he'd done last night, too. "Yeah, same old, same old. Are you saying you didn't pace?"

"All night," he admitted. "Where is he, Kaye?"

* * *

I stepped out of the cold porch turned office into the warmth of the Safe House's living room, expecting to see Flynn and Anita and finish up where we left off. No such luck. The living room was empty except for a blaring TV set playing to a gang of toddlers.

"I had Dina take them out back," Liz's voice came from behind me.

I turned to find her small figure in the doorway, her short light hair mussed but her face calm.

"I have a friend in one of the drug rehab centers who I wanted Anita to talk to and I thought it was better if she could do it in private. So I sent Dina over there with Anita and Flynn to try to make some arrangements."

Translation, Liz had given Dina orders to make sure that Anita dealt with this. The garage-turned-meeting-place/office was definitely more private than anyplace in the house itself. But except for meetings, we usually used it only when a resident had violated some rule and was being asked to leave. Liz must have really wanted to hustle Flynn out.

I raised an eyebrow, wanting to ask the question.

Liz must have read my thoughts. She shrugged. "We're one of the few battered women's shelters who have teenage boys to stay with their mothers anyway. I have to defend that to the board constantly. But I definitely will not tolerate any kind of drug involvement in this house. Anita is welcome to stay but Flynn needs help that we cannot offer here."

Shaking my head ruefully, I said, "I was going to ask you if you knew any counselors who specialized in drug rehab. But frankly I don't want RJ going to the same place as Flynn."

"I have more than one friend," Liz said, smiling blandly, and beckoning me back toward the office. "But first you're going to have to give me more information."

I'd expected that. I followed her back into the cold office, and sat on one of the metal chairs next to her desk. Scrunching my backbone against the chair back, I drew my knees to my chin and took a deep breath. "I was going to tell you before. Dina knows what's going on. But it's all been happening so quickly."

It didn't take long to get the whole story out--Elissa's murder, RJ, the drugs, and confidentially what I knew about Flynn, Josh and Josh's mother. I ended with RJ's run from Bright Harvest. Liz was completely unperturbed--which was probably good since as I retold the whole thing I got more than a little emotional.

"I'm sorry," I said. I took the box of tissues she silently handed me, and hesitated over whether to blow my nose or wipe my almost-definitely, mascara-streaked face first. I settled for a flat hand maneuver that tried to cover both. I looked at Liz over the tissue. "I don't know why I broke down like this."

Her eyes were soft with compassion. "There's something about putting it all into words that makes it more real."

Yes! She understood. A lump rose in my throat and the tears poured harder. Forget the mascara. I blew my dripping nose. "I'm not even sure where to go from here. I can't find RJ. I'm sure that the cops are going to have a fit about this. It makes it look worse for him."

Liz picked up a tissue, leaned over and dabbed at my face. "There's not much you can do about that. RJ made that decision. All you can do is go pick up his stuff, get the lab results on his drug screen, if they have them, and decide what you're going to do with him when you find him." She stopped dabbing and looked me hard in the eyes. "You will find him, Kaye.

He hasn't disappeared from the face of the earth and he hasn't been murdered like Elissa. He's out there, and he'll come back to you."

Until she put it into words, I hadn't realized what I'd been so worried about. But that was it. The last kid who'd gone missing hadn't come back. "Are you sure?"

"Absolutely," she said firmly. "And you need to plan what you're going to do. Get everything lined up now, so you're not taken by surprise. Then when he comes back--whammo. Put him right back in rehab."

I smiled weakly at her force.

She sat back examining her handiwork on my face. Then she patted my hand. "That's good. You take stock and see--it's not as bad as you think. You can actually use this time to plan. And if you take my recommendation, you'll try Genesis Program. It's got a great success rate with teens, and he'll be able to continue his schooling while he's there."

"And you know someone there, so I can get RJ in? Most of these programs have waiting lists."

Liz looked down at her lap and smiled demurely. "I might just have a friend there who owes me a slight favor."

"Okay, if you'll give me a number, I can give them a call later. Roger and I had planned to go over to Bright Harvest together to gather RJ's things after I get done work."

Liz shook her head. "Work? What are you, crazy? This is too much, Kaye. Go home. We can cover for you. You need to get some sleep and find your son and clear all this up. You've got enough personal and comp time coming. And when you're done with that you can use your vacation."

I wasn't going to argue. Lord knew I didn't want to be here. A job was necessary for little things like paying the mortgage and buying groceries. But who wanted any of those things if my kid was in trouble? I was on my way out the door when she stopped me.

"Oh, and Kaye?"

I turned, coat in hand.

"Your instincts about the terrible twosome were right on, too."

I shook my head, not understanding.

"I finally got Darla to break down and tell me what was going on. Martha was going for revenge against her husband. She'd shredded all his shirts, punctured all those tires, and even put sugar in his gas tank."

I gasped. Some women were angry when they got here, and I knew it, but this one was a first.

"Seems he's got a little honey on the side, and Martha could take the years of abuse, but the cheating got to her." Liz's smile was rueful.

I shook my head. "Now what?"

Liz's face turned pensive. "Seems the husband has filed a complaint with the police. Martha is facing a criminal investigation. I imagine they'll be able to sort it out nicely."

I raised my eyebrows. "Yes, I guess so, but should we throw them out?"

"They're already gone. Not that you should worry about that. You just go home and take care of business there."

$* * *$

Home was a still too silent to me. I stood in the front doorway listening to the miserable furnace hum. My need to find RJ was driving me. But where could I go that I hadn't been? Hannah had wanted me to go to Zack's the night before, but I didn't see how RJ could have gone there. I was at Zack's when RJ ran away. Still, it was someplace to go.

Zack poked head and shoulders out the door. His dark eyes were cold and his lips curled down when he saw me.

My polite smile soured inside, but I kept it pasted on anyway. I was driven to that babbling adults do when confronted by a sullen adolescent. "Hey? No school today?"

He shrugged.

"Listen, RJ left rehab last night. Did he come here?"

"He knows better."

What did that mean?

"Zack, who's at the door?" Brenda called from within the house. "Don't you go out! We're due at the lawyers in fifteen minutes."

"Do you know where he went?"

Zack's dark brows met in the center of his face. "Look, you don't get it. RJ won't come here 'cause I'm not goin' to help him. I don't know what happened that day. But we weren't together that whole time. Could be, it went down just like the cops said."

"You mean RJ could have killed Elissa?"

"Shoot, I don't know. It's possible." Zack shrugged and drew out his words. "It's possible."

"Just exactly how long were you away from RJ that afternoon?"

"Look, I'm done with this. I'm doing all my talking to the cops. RJ's nothing but trouble to me. And I don't want more trouble. Now get out. I'm tired of you coming here."

* * *

It had stopped snowing, but the wind was still whipping snow across streets and off rooftops, creating drifts and icy spots. I drove around the school, hoping to find RJ had gone there. Usually, the high school campus and the street around it thronged with teens. But the weather must have been too much for them today. A lone group of kids in sweat suits were doing a lap around the track.

My throat tightened looking at the young athletic forms. I wanted my son. Oh God, where was he? Was he cold? Was he hungry? Did he need...me?

I drove slowly off looking down every side street hoping to see RJ. I kept driving until I found myself at the deserted field where Elissa died. I parked the car off the road and sat staring at the snow whisking across the tall grass and settling in piles against the trees. The car grew cold before I got out. I tromped the length of the field, my shoulders hunched against the wind. Finally I settled on an icy log overlooking the spot where her body had been found.

Elissa hadn't deserved this. She'd been such a sweet little girl. I remembered one day, and it didn't feel that long ago either, when she and Hannah had dressed up in a couple of Thea's old gowns. Giggling, they'd smeared makeup on, and looted my jewelry box for necklaces and all the bracelets their little arms could hold. I'd held my breath looking at both of them, able to see in that moment what beautiful women they would become. Should have both had the chance to become. Oh God.

I still had pictures--somewhere.

The wind whistled desolately through the trees, bringing me back to the field. I'd forgotten both gloves and hat. My hands I could cram in my pocket, but though I tried to pull the collar of my coat up, it wasn't enough. The freezing wind battered my exposed cheeks and ears. I alternately put my hands over my ears and my face trying to protect them. When I couldn't stand the cold anymore or the thought that RJ might be out in it with no coat, I left.

I cranked the car's heat way up and turned the radio on loud to blast over it. Then for lack of a better idea, I patrolled Roger's neighborhood--in case RJ tried to sneak in the empty house for clothes--something I told myself I might do in his place. But he never showed.

Finally, at 2:30, I turned off of Roger's street and decided to stay home. Hannah was due, and it was always possible she had spotted RJ. I must have been home all of a half a minute before the phone rang.

"Kaye? What's going on? I've been trying to catch up with you all day."

Pete. "Hi. Sorry--it's been kind of busy."

"So I gather. RJ ran away from Bright Harvest." Pete's voice was flat.

"How did you know?"

"They filed a runaway report."

He waited for me to say something, but I didn't know what to say.

"They're not happy. It doesn't look good for RJ to be, shall we say, unavailable at this point?"

I didn't think so either although I'd tried to tell myself that RJ's running away had nothing to do with Elissa's murder. I ran my hand through my hair. "Did Deaton tell you that?"

"Yes, and he wanted me to tell you."

"That sounds as though he thinks I know where RJ is."

"Do you?" Pete's voice was cool.

"No and you should know that!"

"Should I? You didn't even call me when you found out RJ was missing."

It was true. I hadn't.

"Maybe we both need time to rethink our relationship, Kaye. I am not going to be satisfied with only being around when there's nothing else better for you to do."

I opened my mouth to protest then shook my head and sighed. I didn't mean to exclude him. I didn't know why I didn't think of him when I got the call from Bright Harvest. I'd needed someone last night. "I'm sorry."

"Is anything else going on? Is there anything I can help you with?"

Yes. Help me find RJ. I had my mouth open to say it. But then I shook my head. What could he do but what I was already doing?

Hannah came in and he twitched her head at the phone as if to ask if I had news. I shook my head at her, and she went downstairs.

To Pete I said, "No, I ... everything's being taken care of."

"Okay." His voice was flat again, and a sigh gusted through the phone line. "I'll have to let you handle this. Call me when you're ready to talk."

I sat at the kitchen table by the phone and stared at the cordless headset in my hand. Before I had a chance to hang it back on the base, it rang again.

"Kaye?"

Mom. "Hi." My voice was quiet even to my own ears.

"What's wrong?"

"Oh, nothing much. It snowed and it's freezing cold and RJ ran away from drug rehab without even a coat. Even I'm beginning to suspect he killed Elissa, and the guy I've been seeing is ready to break up with me because I won't let him into my life."

Being Mom, she went to what really bugged me. "You don't really believe he killed that girl."

"I don't know what to believe."

"What does RJ say?"

"Mom, I told you, RJ ran away."

Patiently she said, "Without his coat. I heard you. What did he tell you before?"

"He said he didn't, of course, but I believed him because he offered to take the cops' blood and hair test."

"Then keep believing."

"Mom, I'm trying, but it's becoming obvious to me that his friends don't believe him. The guy he buys dope from doesn't believe him. Hannah doesn't believe him. And then he ran away from rehab. What does that say? When do you suppose I've got to be realistic? I don't want to support him right into a life of crime. I don't want Jack the Ripper here."

"We're not talking about Jack the Ripper. We're talking about RJ. I know things probably look black now. But, your first reaction was disbelief. RJ couldn't do this. Well, I, for one, don't think you're that out of touch with your child. If you thought he couldn't, he couldn't. You know him best."

"I need to think about that one."

"And don't go beating yourself up over the drugs. You acted as soon as you were sure. Even Pete told you that."

"That'll be the last thing he'll tell me."

"Is there anything else you did wrong? Forgot to hold the world on your shoulders, Miss Atlas?"

I didn't smile. I couldn't, although I knew she meant me to. "Pete was right, if I cared about him, I'd have called."

"Pete was wrong. You didn't even call your own mother. I called you, remember? You've always been independent--thought you should do everything yourself. In my opinion, it's what went wrong in your marriage to Roger--he didn't like independent women. But that's neither here nor there now. You have to concentrate on RJ."

"What do you think I've been doing? I haven't slept in forever. I've looked all over for him, Mom. I can't find him, and you haven't even said anything about him running away." I was so tired, I sagged in the chair.

"What is there to say? He ran away. Your sister skipped out of the first drug counseling place, too. It's not easy. But you need to make up your mind, Katherine. Is RJ so big and scary he killed a girl? Or is he still your little baby lost out there in the snowstorm and not able to take care of himself?"

She waited a moment for me to absorb this, then said. "He'll be all right. But there's something you're missing. It'll come to you, if you keep trying. And when it does, you'll be able to tell them all you were right. RJ didn't do this."

After hanging up with Mom, I called the number Liz had given me for the Genesis Program, not so much because I believed Mom was right and RJ would be back soon, but because I had to do something. All arrangements made, I sat and thought, wondering what it was I knew or Mom thought I knew. No wonderful revelations came to me.

What did come to me was Roger, right on schedule for our four o'clock jaunt to Bright Harvest to pick up RJ's clothes. I called downstairs to Hannah that we were leaving, and walked out to the car.

* * *

Bright Harvest was in an area of downtown Denver that was coming slowly back to life. Streetwalkers mingled with businessmen on the crowded sidewalks. Winos lounged in doorways next to newly remodeled Victorians. Bright Harvest was in one of the Victorians.

Roger eyed the winos and visibly shrank in the driver's seat, obviously worried about his car. Now why hadn't that bothered him before? I considered him thoughtfully, through narrowed eyes. Could it be he hadn't been here before? Then how did RJ's clothes get here in the first place? After all, there had been no time to pack for RJ the night he was brought in.

Knowing Roger, he probably gave RJ's clothes to his secretary to bring over here. And now he was upset at the thought of leaving his car in this neighborhood while he went inside, but he'd left our son here without checking it out.

I smiled at him, showing all my teeth--a sure sign, if he'd noticed, that I was less than happy with him. "Your baby will be fine." I patted the Mercedes' leather seat. Then I got out, leaving him no choice but to lock the car and follow.

The door at Bright Harvest was huge--all heavy oak and brass with an oval etched glass insert. I tried the handle. It was locked. I rang the bell and leaned to peer in the glass. The door opened, and I reared back to keep from falling.

A tall dark-haired woman about my own age with a long face and wire frame glasses gave me a superior smile. "Can I help you?" she asked.

The smile ticked me off. She'd probably seen me peeking in, and opened the door on purpose to put me at a disadvantage. I looked her up and down, pointedly, deciding that her brown herringbone pant suit was a shade too short and that if I had a face that long I'd wear bangs.

From behind me, Roger said smoothly, "We're RJ Atchinson's parents."

The woman's smile never faltered, and she didn't move, merely waiting for him to go on.

I glanced at Roger then said. "I spoke to Lena McQuire last night. She told me RJ ran away. We want to pick up his things and get the results of his drug screen."

"I see." Slowly, the woman opened the door, revealing a beautiful oak staircase rising from a claustrophobically small hall. Oak paneled doors led off from the hall, all of them closed.

"Come in, please." She spoke briskly now, as to a bunch of kindergartners who were dawdling. "I'm Marlene Stephens, assistant administrator here at Bright Harvest." She held out her hand first to Roger, then to me, then took off at a rapid pace up the stairs.

Roger introduced us huffing and puffing his way up the stairs. At the top, Marlene turned left down another dark hallway, the flung open a door to a huge octagonal shaped office. It was flooded with light, in contrast to the hall. I settled in a green padded chair in front of the massive oak desk. Roger stood by the door, uncertainly.

Marlene went immediately to a large black trash bag on the far side of the room, hauling it over the desk. "We will have to ask you to sign a release," she said.

Roger hurriedly stepped forward, taking the bag and some papers from her.

"What's that?" I asked. "Where's RJ's duffel bag?"

Marlene shrugged. "I couldn't tell you that. Possibly your son traded it with the boy whose shoes he took. All I know is, when we went in to gather his clothing from his room, this is what he had. Plus of course, his shoes and coat which we had for safekeeping."

Unless he'd taken the duffel bag with him? I stood and grabbed the bag from Roger, leaving the papers with him. It was unexpectedly heavy. Sitting back down, I pawing through the bag to see what else might be missing. Inside was a jumble of wrinkled clothing. As far as I could tell, the duffel bag was the only thing gone. I looked up at Marlene. "Ms. McQuire gave me no details about why my son might have run away. I was hoping that you could do better." If she got from my tone that I held her responsible, so much the better. But from the expression on her face, I doubted it.

With a bland smile, Marlene spread her hands then sat down slowly. "I have to be completely honest with you. I don't believe that RJ is ready for rehabilitation. It may be that he will have to hit bottom before he is ready to take responsibility for change."

A picture of RJ running from Ken and Roger the night he was brought in flew into my mind. She was right. He didn't want rehab. But her job was to make him want it. "What makes you say that?"

"He was in a group counseling session before lunch. From what I understand, it didn't go well for RJ. The other boys know when someone is being less than completely honest and they tend to call each other on it."

"How was RJ not being honest?" Roger spoke from just behind my chair.

She shrugged. "The counselor reported that RJ was unable to own up to his drug use. The other teens were... perhaps a bit harsh. But we find that peer pressure is effective in these cases. RJ was left alone to think about what had happened in the session. After lunch, the boys have a free period to write in their journal. When it was time for his next counseling session, RJ was not on the grounds."

I drummed my fingers on the desk. There seemed to be no point in asking again how RJ had left. Lena McQuire had made it clear that the facility was not a locked one. As RJ's mother, I wouldn't have left him alone at that point. I'd have made him talk or at least tried to. But these people weren't his mother. And that was at least part of the reason I'd wanted him here. I'd wanted him to have a picture of what he was doing to himself. To see it as the world would.

Sighing, I asked, "Do you have the results of his drug screen?"

She shuffled through a pile of papers on the desk and came up with a manila folder. "Yes, it looks like they're all in," she announced, peering over her glasses at the file.

I wove the strap on my purse in and out of my fingers, waiting for her to tell us more. The tick of the clock on her desk was the only sound. Roger finally sat in the chair next to mine, cast me a sidelong glance, then burst out, "What does it say, for heaven's sake?"

She stared at Roger, arching an eyebrow at his impatience. "For one thing, we found traces of THC in his urine. We do that in-house, so we have the results right away, and it's most likely the reason we admitted him." She flipped through the file, probably searching for his admission sheet.

THC--marijuana. I thought of the pipe full of ashes on his windowsill and sighed. No surprises there, though of course, I'd hoped...

Marlene cleared her throat and went on. "His blood screen also shows a blood alcohol level consistent with legal intoxication."

I met Roger's eyes and nodded. We'd both expected that one, too.

"There are traces of solvents in his blood." This time Marlene's voice sounded heavy.

"Solvents?" Roger asked, eyes bouncing between Marlene and me.

She nodded, her turned down mouth accentuating her long face.

"So you're saying he's sniffing?" I said slowly, trying to piece it together.

"Exactly." She pointed to me with her pen.

"Sniffing? Like glue?" Roger asked. "Kids did that when we were in school."

Marlene consulted her notes. "It's not specific as to what here but what we're typically seeing is something like paint thinner, typewriter correction fluid, cigarette lighter fluid."

Typewriter correction fluid. Oh, God. I remembered the spilled bottle under RJ'S bed. And there were several cigarette lighters floating around that room, too--including the one next to the marijuana pipe. Why hadn't I thought?

Incredibly, Roger laughed. "Typewriter correction fluid?"

Marlene's shook her head. "Typewriter correction fluid. They paint their nails with it and then scratch and sniff it all day. It's a perfect high. No needle tracks, no problems obtaining the stuff. So it's hard for anyone to detect the drug use."

"Wonderful," Roger said. "Still it's not anything like heroine or speed, right? Not really addictive or harmful."

Marlene shrugged. "That's what the abuser will tell you. Most of them don't equate it with drug use. It's just something around the house, right?"

It was dangerous of course. I seemed to remember it being linked to deaths of young kids in Texas and New York. But then again, RJ could OD on alcohol. Kids did that at parties all the time--chugging. And the marijuana wasn't great news either. I sighed and shook my head. "Anything else?"

Marlene browsed through the file, squinting. After a moment she said, "Someone wrote roofies with a question mark in the margin here. It's not clear whether it's part of the lab report or part of the intake."

"Well, find out will you?" My voice was so high it squeaked but I was beyond caring.

Roger's eyes darted from me to Marlene. "What are roofies?"

"Rohypnol," I said, still eying Marlene.

She was oblivious, scanning the pages of RJ's file. I wanted to tear it away from her, and find out what I needed to know myself. If the information was even in there. I faced Roger, his brow still wrinkled as if to ask what the deal was.

Taking a deep breath to try to calm myself, I said, "Kids use Rohypnol with alcohol sometimes to increase the drunken feeling. It's cheap--looks kind of legal because it comes in those little bubble packages."

Roger nodded. He knew what I meant.

"But it's scary stuff, and kids can have seizures or convulsions when they try to stop."

I watched Marlene, trying to hurry her in her inspection of the file.

She glanced up and caught me at it, then considered Roger. "You've probably heard of it. It's been in the news as a date rape drug."

"Oh, God," Roger said. "Yes, I've heard of it." His eyes met mine. "You don't think... Elissa?"

Chapter 18

"I don't know what to think any more," I said. "It might explain why her assailant showed no signs of a struggle..."

"Of course, Elissa doesn't necessarily have to have taken it even if RJ..." Roger said.

"Of course," I agreed.

Marlene looked from one of us to the other. "I'm afraid I don't understand."

I shook my head, standing and handing the trash bag to Roger. "Sorry, we were talking about something else. Is there any way you could get back to me with information on the Rohypnol?"

Marlene rose also. "I will certainly do my best to track down the source of that note. The counselor who did the intake is unavailable. But I will speak to her tonight and get back to you as soon as possible."

Back in his unblemished car, Roger turned to me. "Now what?"

Did I look like I had all the answers? I couldn't deal with any of this anymore. I hunched a shoulder, tired, then slouched back in the seat and closed my eyes. "You've got me. Any ideas on where he might be?"

"If I'd had any ideas to begin with, I'm all out by now."

That pretty well summed it up. I nodded, eyes still closed. "I guess I'll just go home."

Roger drove away before I even got in the door away from the icy wind. I set the heavy bag of RJ's clothes down by the door. The house felt warm, and Hannah had her music blaring again. Not that I cared. After days of silence, the music was a blessing. I checked my watch. Only 5:30. I really should rustle up something for our dinner. With a guilty eye on the stairway that led to Hannah's room, I promised myself that I would. I really would make dinner in just a minute. But first, I just wanted to sit, not for long, just a little bit. I slumped on the couch and pulled the knit afghan over me..

"Mom!" Hannah's voice was an urgent whisper. Her hands on my shoulders were rough. "Wake up. Someone's in the house."

What? I bolted upright, finding myself on the couch still in my coat, covered by a comforter. The room was dark. Hannah was in footed pj's, her tousled. "What time is it?"

"I don't know. After midnight sometime--who cares? Mom, you have to get up. Someone's in the house."

I raised one eyebrow. "Are you sure you weren't having a nightmare?"

Hannah put her fingers to her lips. "Listen."

Obediently, I shut up. The furnace hummed, and Hannah's music still thumped. What did she expect me to hear over that? I got up, letting my afghan slip to the floor and walked softly to the window. No sign of any kind of a vehicle out front. If this was RJ, he didn't have any transportation. Or said transportation was smart enough to park out of sight. It was hot in here. I tugged off the rumpled coat, ready to hang it in the closet. A muffled thud from the basement made me drop the coat and whirl to meet Hannah's frightened eyes. She hadn't dreamed it.

My adrenalin was running high now, but I wasn't scared. It had to be RJ, and if I didn't play this right, I might miss my chance. Moving back to Hannah, I whispered in her ear. "Take the cordless phone into my room and call your father, and Pete-- his number is in the phone book. Then call Liz and tell her I called her friend but I need help tonight. She'll know what to do."

I moved to the stairs, but Hannah lunged and grabbed my arm. "Mom, are you crazy? You're acting like that's RJ down there. It's not. It's probably one of his stoner friends."

I turned to face her. "What makes you say that?"

"If it were RJ, he'd have woken me up. I am his sister, you know."

Smiling, I answered, "I seem to remember that." Reaching out to smooth her hair I said, "I'll be careful. But if it's RJ, I need to be ready for him. So I'm depending on you to call out the cavalry."

"And if it's not RJ?"

I did have to consider that. My gut was telling me it was my kid down there, but guts could be wrong. "Hey, if you hear me yell, feel free to call the police."

As I slowly slipped down the darkened stairway, I tried to decide what to say if it was RJ. Why did you run away? What are you doing? Or how about--I threw out your stash, don't bother looking.

A flickering light led me directly to his room, strengthening me in the belief that it had to be my son. Besides, who else could it be? Flynn was in rehab himself by now, hopefully a lock-down facility, as Lena McQuire would put it. And Zack said he wasn't going to help RJ anymore. Elissa was dead. That thought made me quieter. After all, whoever had broken into my house could be her killer.

I eased open RJ's bedroom door and stood watching a minute. A thin figure in a black hooded sweatshirt was pushing clothes into a couple of plastic grocery bags by the light of a white column-shaped candle.

"None of your favorite clothes are here, son. I just got them back from Bright Harvest tonight and haven't had time to bring them down."

RJ turned toward my voice, seemingly unsurprised to see me. His eyes looked red even in the small amount of light in the room. He moved to the door, close enough for me to smell him. He reeked of sweat and something else--a chemical odor. "I've got enough."

I wanted to hug him, shake him, tell him how much I missed him and worried about him, but sensed that he would reject any movement that I made that way. My alarm bells were going off loudly. I had to keep him here until Roger or Pete got here. RJ was on something and, from the smell of him, I suspected maybe solvents. He needed help.

I moved past him to sit on the bed, hoping to prolong the discussion. "Enough for what? Where are you going?" I patted a space on the bed next to me, hoping he'd come sit down.

He ignored the gesture, choosing instead to lean against the doorframe. "Enough."

"Why are you doing this? Was Bright Harvest that bad?"

"Bright Harvest was a freakin' joke. I don't need that shit. I'm not some stoned out freak."

"RJ, you smoke marijuana, you sniff typewriter correction fluid and cigarette lighter fluid. Do you know how dangerous that stuff can be?"

His face twisted up in violent rejection. "You think that's bad? That's nothing. I don't do speed, or heroin, or any of that crap. I'm not addicted to anything. Typewriter correction fluid--if it's so bad then every secretary in America is in trouble. Gee, I'm scared."

The overhead light flashed on.

"You should be." Pete's voice came from the doorway. He looked so comfortingly solid. "The police are actively looking for you now."

RJ's eyes widened and his mouth made a small oh, whether at Pete's presence or what he'd said, I didn't know. I took a deep breath, trying not to show my tension. After all, Pete got here quickly; surely Roger couldn't be far behind. RJ would be all right. He'd see sense. Or we'd take him into rehab anyway. It would work out.

"Do you have any idea how bad it looked for you when you ran?" Pete asked. "Now they think you're the one who beat Elissa up."

"Like I would." RJ gave an unconvincing but angry laugh.

"Yeah, so who would? Zack?" I asked. "He told me you guys weren't together all afternoon."

RJ's eyes swung toward me, his expression blank. This was evidently a new idea. Slowly he said, "Maybe. He was always kind of pissed 'cause she wouldn't do him. Figured she was a racist." He shook his head, smiling a little at the memory. "I told him 'Lissa wasn't like that. She just thought he was a little kid, you know? Didn't want him involved in that whole mess." His eyes focused and narrowed at me. "She was trying to get off drugs, you know. She'd gotten into some pretty hard stuff, but she was getting off."

I nodded, trying to smile a little, as though this was just small talk. "So I heard. Did that make Flynn mad?"

"What is it with you about Flynn? That's so messed up. He didn't do this. He loved Elissa. If anybody beat her up, it was her Mom. She was there that day, you know."

A piece of the puzzle plopped into place. Mom was right after all. I did know something I hadn't thought of. RJ's backpack had always puzzled me. Flynn said Elissa had had it. But if that was so, why didn't RJ tell the cops that? I nodded. "She brought Elissa the backpack, didn't she? Did Elissa leave it at home?"

"Yeah, God, was her Mom pissed! Elissa put some dope in it. Nothing much, some marijuana and some roofies. But her mom went nuts."

Roofies, Rohypnol. Well, I didn't have to wait for the call from Bright Harvest to confirm that one. I sighed.

"So why didn't you tell the police that her mom had the backpack?" Pete's voice startled me.

He'd moved into the room past RJ, in front of the window. Catching my eyes, he jerked his head toward the window. Someone was out there. Roger?

RJ said, "I didn't want to get into the whole thing--if I told about Elissa's mom, then this whole drug thing would come out. I didn't want to end up in jail because of her."

Pete nodded understandingly. He deliberately locked his gaze on mine then moved his eyes toward the door. When I didn't immediately move, he lifted his chin up high, scratching it thoughtfully, then jerked it toward the door.

All right. I should get RJ ready to leave. I got off the bed. But I still had a question I had to ask. "RJ, that day--you were irritable and spaced out. Were you and Elissa sniffing something in the field?"

"What if we were?"

What if they were? It was a thought I couldn't deal with now--except that I had to. "RJ, I've made arrangements for you to go to another drug rehab program."

"That's jacked up. I'm not going to any more..."

Roger strode into the room, his face red with cold or anger. I couldn't tell. "You'll go where we tell you."

"You think?" RJ laughed that angry laugh again. "You think just because you got me trapped in this room with three of you, I'm going to do what you want? You better think again. I got friends right outside, and I'm not going anywhere I don't want to go."

I twisted around to face the window, squinting hard to try to see past the black surface reflecting only us on the inside of the room. That was what Pete had been trying to say. He must have seen RJ's friends when he came in. Now what? I took another deep breath, released it and swung back to face RJ. Pete caught my eye and gave a brief headshake.

What did that mean? Had he chased the other kids away? Or did he just mean that if I stared out there, the other kids would come in? I picked at my watchband, considering what to say.

Roger had no such inhibition. He lunged toward RJ and made a grab for his arm. "Your friends better come in, if they're going to stop me, son. I told you when you went to Bright Harvest, and I'm telling you now, no kid of mine is going to do drugs."

"Maybe I don't want to be a kid of yours, okay? I want to do more with my life than live in some big stuck-up house and screw around on my wife." RJ swung his arm up to hit his dad, squirming away.

Roger's face froze but he grabbed RJ's fist before it had a chance to connect. This was getting out of hand. And if RJ did have friends outside, the odds might not be in our favor. I stood and eased around the two, heading for the door.

"Whether you want to be or not, you're my son." Roger's voice was low and hoarse with emotion. "And I'm not going to let you do drugs."

"Maybe there's nothing you can do about that."

But there was. I never thought I'd have to do it, but I would. I stepped quietly out into the rec room, grabbed the phone and dialed the police.

* * *

There was no sign when I came back into the room that anyone had moved. RJ, his fists tightly clenched, stood breathing heavily into Roger's face. Roger's grip on RJ's arm looked tight. His brows made one heavy dark line across his forehead, his jaw jutted out. Pete stood poised, ready to intervene if necessary.

I crammed myself in between Roger and RJ. "This has to stop."

RJ shoved me hard. Caught off guard, I felt myself falling toward the bed. My shoulder hit his wooden headboard hard. I would have a bruise from that one.

Pete dove to right me, then whirled to face RJ, his face cold. In a whisper, he said, "You do not touch your mother."

"She shouldn't have gotten in the way." RJ's breathing was alarmingly heavy now.

God, we had to get him somewhere. His increasing aggression scared me, but not any more than that breathing. And he'd admitted to the rohypnol. They'd been in his backpack that night. I wanted help. Then it hit me. Was this how it had been the night Elissa died? RJ had admitted they had been sniffing something. Had Elissa had respiratory problems? The autopsy should reveal some of this, maybe already had. But what caused the bleeding? Who had beaten her? God! RJ had just pushed me and he'd tried to hit his father. He couldn't...

A loud banging on the front door interrupted my thoughts. RJ's friends wouldn't bother knocking. I bolted for the stairs, bounding up to the front door with my heart in my throat.

"Come in, officer," I told the waiting cop.

He hesitated. "My backup has circled around the back-- dispatch said you thought he might have a friend back there?"

I nodded. "He claimed to. But I haven't seen anyone. He's getting violent, though."

The cop nodded and stepped in, moving with me toward the stairs. "You've got this set up with the drug rehab center?"

Hannah called tearfully from the doorway to my room "Liz called back to say that they're waiting for him at Genesis house, but they can't transport him so they're asking for an ambulance."

"Thanks, honey. I appreciate your help. But I don't want you to be part of this," I said, waving her back into my room. To the cop I said, "Is that okay?"

"Normally we call the ambulance in these cases, and if need be, help them restrain him. But I've been told that Detective Deaton has a special interest in this case, and has asked that we transport ourselves."

"Actually, I'm worried about his breathing. I'd like to have the ambulance."

He nodded and spoke into his radio. When he got done, he said shortly to me, "We'll escort."

I nodded, heart heavy. Deaton wanted to be sure where RJ was. Not good news surely. Another thought to shelve for when I could worry about it. Crashing noises from downstairs indicated that the conflict was not over. The cop followed me into the room.

RJ's bedroom floor was littered with clothes and CDs again--this time stuff knocked over in the struggle. In the middle of the carpet, Roger attempted to sit on RJ's kicking feet. Pete sat on RJ's back, straining to hold RJ's floundering arms. He nodded when he saw who was with me.

"RJ, stop," I said. "Please. There is someone here to see you."

RJ looked from me to the officer, arching his back. "You called the cops on me? I can't believe you. These guys jump me, and you call the cops on me. This is abuse."

The cop's radio let out a burst of static. He unhooked it from his belt and said something into it.

RJ screamed. "Do you freakin' hear me? This is abuse! I don't have to take this crap. I've got rights."

The cop nodded to Pete and Roger who both responded by standing up. Then in one seemingly fluid motion, the cop hauled RJ upright and snapped handcuffs on him. "Your rights do not include the ability to get high. Your parents have requested help transporting you to rehab, and I'm here to give them that help."

"You can't do this. I've got rights," RJ screamed.

I took a long shuddering breath, ready to explain to the cop that RJ was under fifteen. But explanations seemed unnecessary; the cop ignored RJ and spoke instead into his radio. A loud thud from the vicinity of the utility room suggested that the other cops had found the garden level door open and were coming in to check things out. I heard footsteps, then a tall dark haired older officer walked into the room, and raised an eyebrow to the other policeman. "Everything okay?"

"I've got this one," said the cop holding RJ.

The older one said, "The back yard appears to be clear, but that doesn't mean someone wasn't there. The snow out there is pretty trampled. We can do increased patrols of the neighborhood tonight. Just to see if anyone comes back."

"Please," I said simply.

"Okay." The cop led RJ forward. "We need to transport to Genesis house. Apparently, all the arrangements have been made."

"Actually," I cleared my throat and looked at Roger. "One of us will have to sign him in."

He nodded. "I'll do it. I know where it is."

"Mom," said RJ, his eyes pleading.

"RJ, you need help. Please, please, try to stay with this program."

His eyes filled with tears. "I don't want to go anywhere. I want to stay here. Please."

I wanted to pull him onto my lap the way I did when he was little and kiss him and make it all better. But I knew I couldn't. My chest hurt, and my throat felt so raw with unshed tears, I couldn't speak. I shook my head.

Roger said quietly, "It will be all right, son. Your mother and I will come to visit as soon as they let us."

"You're going to need these," Pete said holding out the grocery bags stuffed with clothes.

RJ wagged his cuffed hands behind his back, a disgusted look on his face. Roger said, "I'll take them."

RJ shook his head, but he walked quietly up the steps with the officers, looking back at me pleadingly over his shoulder. I followed them up and walked them out the front door. He looked so thin, so young so... vulnerable. Was this the right thing to do? Maybe RJ would be better off in an outpatient program where he could at least come home every day. I felt so tired, so drained. I watched from the threshold, as the cops put RJ in the back of the squad car.

Roger dropped the grocery bags and put his arm around my shoulders. "We'll get through this, you know."

He hadn't hugged me since before the divorce. I stepped back a little-- feeling my eyes mist.

"We did good," he said. "This had to happen."

He sounded so sure. I wished I could feel that way. But I sniffed and nodded.

"Really, Kaye, you'll see. RJ needed to have the message that we wouldn't tolerate the drugs. Now that he's got it, the ball is his, but I think he'll run with it." With a quick nod at Pete who stood still in the stairway door watching, Roger picked up RJ's clothes and left.

Run with it? He'd run all right. That was RJ's answer to the first drug rehab place. What made us think that this place would be different? But Roger was gone.

Clearing my throat, I looked at Pete and said, "Thanks. I wasn't sure you would come."

He raised an eyebrow. "You weren't?"

"No. How did you get here so fast?"

"I was already in the car on the way here, when I got Hannah's call. I wanted to talk to you."

I nodded, not looking at him now, not asking why he would decide to talk to me in the middle of the night. I looked instead at my feet, drawing a line on the carpet with my shoe. "I don't think I can right now."

"I'm not dumb, Kaye."

His voice sounded amused, surprising me. I looked up.

"I was just glad you had Hannah call me." He smiled.

"I can't promise..."

He stretched out a hand, pulling me down on the couch with him, tucking me under his arm. "We'll talk later, when this has all calmed down," he said, laying his cheek on my head. "Maybe we can get some time together over the holiday weekend."

Holiday? Thanksgiving. Him and Dina. I didn't even want to begin to think of that now. But Hannah deserved some kind of celebration. And so did Pete. I said, "You want to go to Thanksgiving dinner over at Dina's with us?" I twisted around to look up at him, not sure of what I was saying with the invitation. "I mean..."

"I know. Just to eat. It sounds good." He stood up, tugging on my hand to pull me close again. "Maybe you and Hannah should go there now."

"No!" I pushed away from him, startled to hear it to come out as forcefully as that. But I wasn't going to skulk at Dina's tonight--worrying. I had to finish this. Carefully I said, "Everything will be fine. The cops checked the neighborhood. There's nobody here. And if there is, I've got a phone."

He nodded and walked toward the door, then stopped and strode back across the room. He pulled me quickly into his arms, gave me a hard kiss and let me go. "Something else to think about tonight," he said.

Closing my eyes, and sinking against the cushions of the couch, I heard his footsteps, the squeak of the front door and the thud of its closing. He wasn't kidding. Something to dream about. I would think about it--later. Right now, I was going to drop Hannah off at Dina's.

I thought briefly about pounding on Brenda's door and demanding to talk to Zack. But he was more involved with this than he'd admitted. I couldn't count on hearing the truth from him. And I had to know.

So I decided. I didn't care what time it was. I didn't care about any threats. I was going to talk to Thea again. She was the only one who might be able to confirm what I thought I knew. And I needed confirmation. I wanted this over.

Chapter 19

No lights were on at the Pappas' house. The snow had finally stopped, and I sat uneasily in the cold car. I should have called. I could still wait until tomorrow. After all, the information wouldn't change. But I had to know. I had to get this over.

The doorbell echoed in the quiet night. Finally, after what seemed like forever, the front porch light flashed on, and I saw an eye peering at me from through the peephole in the door. Then a short, pudgy figure in plaid pajamas and a black silk bathrobe cracked open the door. His graying chest hair poked out of the deep vee of the bathrobe.

George... God, was I glad to see him. Maybe now we could get this whole thing out in the open.

"Kaye? Is something wrong?"

"I need to talk to you and Thea," I said.

His brows met over his eyes, as he surveyed me in silence. George Pappas and I had known each other a long time, and I knew that most of our mutual friends considered him and Thea to be somewhat of an odd couple. Gorgeous as Thea was, she could have anyone. No one considered George gorgeous. Despite that, I knew Thea was the lucky one in this marriage. The man was just plain good--the kind you'd want on your side when you were in a tight corner. I'd never seen him turn anyone away, and I was counting on that now.

Still silent, he swung the door wide. Thea stood at the top of the stairs; her tall shape encased in a long, gray T-shirt. I was shocked at how thin she looked.

"I told you not to come here," she said, starting down the stairs.

I stepped forward to meet her, deciding to plunge right in. "Yes, you did. But I have more to worry about than whether George knows you're drinking."

George's swiftly indrawn breath told me what a shock this was, but I never switched my scrutiny from his wife's face. Her shoulders slumped and she bit her lip as her eyes searched for his. She wasn't going to deny it. Part of me wanted to look back at George to see if he could accept her. But that was something they could work out on their own. I still needed to know so much. I could not allow this tangent. "What blood type are you?"

"What?" Thea stammered.

"What blood type was Elissa?" I changed the question, hoping to come at the problem from another angle.

"As if it mattered now." Thea slumped down to sit on the steps, arms wrapped around herself as though she were cold.

"It does. I want to know whose blood that is on the backpack."

George stepped forward. "Elissa was type A. Same as me."

"And what are you?" I turned to Thea.

"What is this, the inquisition? George let you in, but that doesn't mean I have to answer your stupid questions."

I looked at George. "Thea was there that night. I already know that. RJ told me."

"RJ," Thea spat the name.

"I also know that you and Elissa were arguing because you had found RJ's backpack here, and it was full of drugs."

George's round face suddenly looked pinched and older. "Thea is a type O."

"O is what they found on the pack," I said softly.

"So you're trying to get your son off the hook, by saying it's Elissa's blood on the backpack and that I killed her."

"Not at all. I'm just trying to get to the bottom of this."

"Right!"

"Thea, I need to know. Please, RJ said he left."

"And you believed him?" Thea's voice was scornful.

I met her eyes, needing her to see I wasn't out to get her. Needing her to see my need to know. Hoping only that she would take pity on that.

"I don't know what to believe. I know he and Elissa were sniffing something in the field. He told me that."

"You got that right. Not just sniffing stuff, you should see what I found in that backpack."

"So you were there but you left? If you know more, I need to know. I have to know what happened."

"You want to hear what happened? Elissa pushed me. She hit me with the backpack." Thea's voice rang with outrage.

And Thea had been angry, was still angry. Hadn't I just felt that way myself with RJ? Suddenly, I doubted my theory again.

More slowly she said, "You're right. It's my blood on it. But I didn't do anything."

"Nothing? Are you sure? Were you drinking that day? Maybe you blacked it out."

Thea's face whitened making her eyes look like huge, haunted black holes. Her mouth thinned in an effort to keep it from trembling. "I worried about that," she said in a hoarse whisper, hunching over and rubbing her face with her hands. "It's happened. I have had blackouts. But I don't think I could ever hurt her." Her head snapped back up, her face contorted, she said, "I wouldn't. You're just trying to make RJ look innocent."

"Thea, listen to me. I need to know. Are the drug screens in yet?"

Thea shook her head, and put her hands over her ears. "I'm not listening to another thing from you."

"George, tell me, please."

"Kaye, I don't understand. You come here in the middle of the night, you accuse my wife of killing our daughter and now you want to know if Elissa's drug screens are in."

"George, I haven't accused Thea of anything. I know it looks that way, and I'm sorry about exposing her drinking to you. I know that was a shock, but I need to know. Surely with the autopsy they told you, her injuries didn't kill her, did they?"

"No," he said slowly. "The drug screens aren't in yet. The cops thought at first--she did have a wound on the side of her head. She didn't look like herself at all--that's why we had a closed casket. But now they're saying they don't think her injuries were the cause of death." He stopped and gathered himself together, running a hand through his hair. "That's not what you were saying though. You're right, her injuries, the blood loss, the hypothermia don't seem like enough. They are checking her blood to see if she took something, maybe overdosed on something. But the cops didn't know that at first. All they saw was this dead girl with an injured head. For all they knew, it was a skull fracture."

"Wait. Back up. The cops found her dead?"

George nodded, brows knit together. "That's right."

"That's not what you said, Thea." I turned and squatted down in front of her, pulling her hands off her ears. "You told me she recognized you."

"I don't know what you're talking about."

"Oh, yes, you do. You called me the night after Elissa died. You said they'd found her. You told me she opened her eyes and recognized you."

"Kaye," George reached out to take Thea's hands from me. "Thea couldn't have. Elissa was pronounced dead at the scene."

"I know what she told me, George." I turned back to Thea, grabbing her shoulders and looking her in the eyes. "I can remember that conversation word for word. She looked at you, you said, with those big eyes that just said Mama help me."

Thea's mouth worked silently, her eyes brimmed with tears.

"Thea, you *were* there when she died, weren't you?"

The tears slid silently down her cheeks, her whole body shuddered, her nose ran. "I never touched her. She just sort of fell, and hit her head. There was blood all over, but they said the injury couldn't have killed her. I never--I swear--I didn't black out. RJ killed her."

Despite the fact that she'd tried to blame this on my son, my heart twisted in compassion for her. Instead of the relief I'd expected to feel with this confirmation of my theory, I felt drained, and exhausted--and heartbroken for her. Softly, I said, "No, Thea, I believe you. You didn't touch her. I know that. But you have to tell the police what really happened. They need to know the truth. She stopped breathing then, didn't she? RJ wasn't there. She hit her head as she went down, and stopped breathing."

"What the hell are you two talking about?" George turned on Thea, grabbing her away from me and shaking her. "You did this? You blamed RJ and, all the while, you killed our daughter?"

"George." I tried to grab his arm, to stop him but his grip was iron hard.

Thea flopped in his grasp like a rag doll.

"George!" This time I shouted, needing somehow to break through. "She didn't do it. You said it yourself. Elissa died of the drug--whatever she was sniffing."

He kept it up, seeming not to hear me, his face intently fixed on his wife's.

I pounded on his arms. "George, stop! Elissa had a heart attack."

He stopped abruptly, and the room was so quiet, his breathing rasped loudly. His hands still grasping her arms, they both turned toward me, their mouths identical ohs, their eyes wide.

Thea found her voice first. "She was fourteen, Kaye."

I nodded. "I know. But that's the danger with these kinds of drugs. The kids get startled or revved up with exercise." I shivered. "And the heart can't take it. They're dead."

Chapter 20

The sweet smell of cinnamon and apples wafted over Dina's house. Silver threads gleamed in the white tablecloth that covered her dining table. Candles flickered behind hurricane glass and sparkled on mirrored trays brightening the gray day.

It was beautiful, and I knew I was lucky to have a friend who would go to such effort for us. If only RJ... But Genesis house was making no exceptions for the holiday. Since he'd run from the previous program, they were being even more cautious. They wouldn't allow him visitors until next week. I bit my lip at the thought of him there alone on Thanksgiving.

I knew it was the right thing to do. I knew he'd be all right and this was only for a little while. But it broke my heart. I took a deep breath to try to pull myself together. Better drug rehab and RJ alive somewhere even if not with me, than dead and cold like Elissa. I couldn't even imagine what George and Thea's Thanksgiving must be like. And it was time for me to remember my other child who had a definitely sulky expression on her face. I leaned over to whisper in Hannah's ear. "Dina really put herself out for dinner."

"Yeah, but it's Thanksgiving. Why can't we have turkey?" Hannah whispered back.

"Aren't you too old to whine like this?" I asked. "You can have turkey later with your father."

Pete, who had been looking out the window, turned and grinned. If the idea of a vegetarian Thanksgiving bothered him, he didn't show it.

"Yeah, like I want to eat two Thanksgiving dinners," Hannah said.

Dina, who had refused all help, bustled into the room with a basket of flaky rolls and a huge Waldorf salad, a bottle of champagne clamped under her arm. A white apron covered her flowing ethnic print dress.

I shook my head at Hannah and whispered, "Think of this as a late lunch and the one with your Dad as dinner." To Dina, I said, "I wish you'd let us help."

She shook her head. "You just sit. I've got it all worked out. The soufflé should be coming out of the oven when we've finished eating the salad course. And all the side dishes are ready and waiting."

Setting down the rolls and salad, she handed the wine with a flourish to Pete. "Will you do the honors, please? There's a towel on the sideboard there to help you grip it." She nodded to show him where. Over her shoulder she called, "Phil, I forgot the champagne glasses."

"No problem." Phil burst out of the kitchen, the delicate stems of the champagne glasses grasped firmly in his huge hands. His grin lit his face as brightly as the candles lit the room and his balding head gleamed in the light. There was nothing Phil liked better than a party. He rumbaed over to the sideboard to set the glasses down. Just seeing him made me feel better.

"I still don't understand all this, Kaye," Dina said, finally sitting down. "You're saying that Elissa's mom was there when Elissa died?"

"Yeah, and if nobody killed her, why didn't the cops say so?" Hannah sounded genuinely bewildered.

I shrugged. "At first, they didn't know. Elissa was dead--apparently under violent circumstances."

Pete grunted from the other side of the room where he had the champagne bottle between his legs as he and Phil both tugged on the cork. "You have to remember, Hannah, that Elissa did have that wound on her face. For all they knew she had a fractured skull."

"But they should have figured that out pretty soon," Hannah said.

"The autopsy results took a couple of days to come back, and when they did, all the coroner could say was that her heart had stopped. He could speculate about the cause, of course, but it all depended on the test results."

"But how long does it take to do a urine analysis?" Dina asked skeptically.

I shook my head. "No time at all, we both know that. But the u/a showed only the marijuana--so that didn't help. Arvada P.D. sent the blood toxicology screen to the state's crime lab. But they had a back load of cases. All of this takes time. It took a bit to get the results."

"So the cops didn't know anything except that she was dead," Hannah said.

I nodded. "And that she shouldn't be. If drugs were involved, it just made more questions. Was it something in the drugs? Or maybe an overdose? They wanted to find her supplier. And her wounds clouded the whole thing, too. So they needed to find out what happened in the field that day. And RJ and Zack were there."

"Could it still be an overdose?"

"I don't think so, honey. RJ pretty well admitted he and Elissa had sniffed something that night. And when I finally got Thea to go to the cops with her story, they seemed to think it all hung together with the other evidence."

"But RJ could still be in trouble as her supplier."

Pete shook his head, his face red from his exertions with the champagne. "Elissa bought the stuff herself, remember? She's the one who put it in the backpack."

"The backpack is what made it all so messed up. I couldn't see how a backpack could kill anybody, but the papers said it," Hannah said.

"The cops don't tell the papers everything. They don't want to tip their hands." Pete said. "Often the media takes what little it does know and blows it up."

"And Thea's story just seemed to back the paper up," I said sadly.

"Yes, I wonder why she did that," Hannah said. "I thought she liked us."

"She was upset," I said slowly. "Anyone would be. She'd watched her daughter die. And she couldn't quite convince herself that she didn't do it. And if she couldn't convince herself..."

"Who knew what the police would think?" Pete finished my thought.

The cork popped, and Phil dove away from the spurting champagne bottle, laughing.

"Well, you can excuse her, Kaye," Dina said, standing up from the table and crossing the room to supervise the pouring of the champagne. "But I don't think I'd ever be able to forgive her if I were in your shoes. She had even you wondering if RJ did this."

Phil reached under the sideboard and grabbed a bottle of sparkling grape juice, hoisting it toward Hannah with a smile. She nodded, grinning as he poured it in a champagne glass for her. They had thought of everything.

I shook my head at Dina. "RJ was the one who had me wondering. After all my training, I didn't know how to react to his drug problem."

Dina paused in carrying wine glasses to the table, and met my eyes. "You know you did the right thing."

Did I? But I wanted him with me for Thanksgiving. I missed him so much. My throat tightened and tears welled as I pictured him sitting at some long institutional-type table eating overdone turkey and dry stuffing.

"You need to take care of yourself now, too," Dina said.

"I am," I said, swallowing the lump in my throat, and blinking back my tears.

"Are you?" Dina cocked an eyebrow.

Surprisingly, Hannah backed me up. "She is. She even finally bought a bed for her room."

"Oh, really?" said Pete.

I put my chin up and looked at him, warning him with my eyes not to read anything into that. "It was about time. I've been sleeping on a cot since my divorce."

"A toast," Phil proclaimed, raising his champagne glass. "To taking care of ourselves and doing the right thing at the right time."

"Hear, hear," said Pete, smiling.

I reached for my glass. With a clatter of chairs, Hannah and Pete both stood up and pulled me out of my chair, each wrapping an arm around me. Then in unison, we raised our glasses.

The End

If you enjoyed this author's book, then please place a review up at the site of purchase, and any social media sites you frequent!

You can find ALL our books our website at:

https://www.writers-exchange.com

All Christine's Books:

https://www.writers-exchange.com/Christine-Duncan/

All our mysteries:

https://www.writers-exchange.com/category/genres/mystery-thrillers-suspense/

About the Author

Christine Duncan is the author of the Kaye Berreano mystery series. Safe House is the second book in the series. Christine resides in Colorado with her husband and children.

You can keep track of her books on her author page:

https://www.writers-exchange.com/Christine-Duncan/

If you want to read more about books by this author, they are listed on the following pages...

The Kaye Berreano Mystery Series

Battered women's shelter counsellor Kaye Berreano searches out the complexities of minds and hearts...along with solving the seemingly never-ending mysteries that keep cropping up around her.

Book 1: Safe Beginnings

When the fire alarm at a battered women's shelter goes off, counselor Kaye Berreano rushes to evacuate the residents, but she's too late. Her patient Mary Ellen is dead. Farrell, the skeptical arson investigator, believes Kaye knows who set the fire.

Farrell's main theory is that Mary Ellen, in a moment of suicidal crisis, set the fire herself. Kaye knows Mary Ellen was *not* suicidal.

Kaye launches her own investigation while dealing with Farrell, attending to her divorce and caring for two teenagers. From a roommate who fought with Mary Ellen, to another patient at the shelter who's in the safe house mistakenly by court order, to a fanatical minister from Mary Ellen's church who doesn't believe in divorce for any reason, Kaye discovers suspects and motives aplenty...while the truth remains just out of reach.

Publisher: https://www.writers-exchange.com/safe-beginnings/

Book 2: Safe House

With snow falling and Thanksgiving coming up fast, Colorado is plunged into a winter wonderland. Battered women's counselor Kaye Berreano doesn't have time to celebrate. She has two teens at home that tend to claim most of her attention along with a new relationship with police investigator Pete Farrell. Already feeling overwhelmed, Kaye isn't sure she can take much more when a kid she's known since birth turns up dead and her own son RJ becomes a suspect. Forced into an investigation, she's led from the safe house...to her own house.

Publisher: https://www.writers-exchange.com/safe-house/